THE
CYBERENE

By
ROG PHILLIPS

I0541408

ARMCHAIR FICTION
PO Box 4369, Medford, Oregon 97504

MANKIND VERSUS THE MACHINE!

Somewhere in the future, a diabolical brain was plotting the enslavement of mankind. The irony being, of course, that it was man who orchestrated the surreptitious take over in the first place! Out of the future and into the past comes a sentient being that has been gaining knowledge and abilities for over a thousand years. A growing monstrosity bent on controlling not only the human condition in its own time, but manipulating the human mind in our time as well.

Armed with knowledge of mankind's sterile future, Earl Frye sets out to do battle against man's ultimate creation—changing an unforeseen destiny!

FOR A SECOND COMPLETE NOVEL, TURN TO PAGE 89

CAST OF CHARACTERS

DR. VICTOR GLASSMAN
Inventor of the Brain—a massive computer project just waiting to be lit up. Would it be everything he'd hoped for?

ETHEL GLASSMAN
She was afraid. She didn't know what this contraption was that her husband had engineered…or what it would it be capable of.

EARL FRYE
A very busy scientist, he had little time for outside enterprise. Now he was expected to save the human race too?

NADINE HOLMES
Naked, blue, and only four inches tall, this little bombshell was about to turn science, and Earl's life, on its ear!

BASIL NELSON
Earl's right-hand man, he was ready to do his duty in whatever manner it needed to be done—right to the nitty-gritty end.

GEORGE LADD
He was a little green companion to Nadine, the "heavy" to her "soft." And he was not as open-minded as his partner was.

IRENE CONNER
Brilliant, curvy, and sassy—this was one lab assistant anyone would want on their payroll. Aye Karumba!

CHAPTER ONE

"VICTOR!" Her voice shattered the cathedral silence, going the full four hundred and fifty-foot perimeter of the fourteen-foot wide floor that encircled the case of the *Brain*. The echo rebounded from the maze of ladders and catwalks that went up and up until they were lost to view where the fifteen-foot thick outer wall began its upward slope to form the giant dome.

The silence returned; as motionless as the needles on the instrument panels resting on their zero pegs, unactivated; as enduring in essence as the atom proof concrete dome built to last—as long as the Earth itself.

Then—a sound answered. A faint sound. Footsteps. Movement appeared through the grillwork of steel catwalks above. Trousered legs. A hand sliding along a railing of chrome pipe. More rapid steps as the man descended a steep stair well. Sharper as the man reached the marble floor.

Dead video camera eyes let his passage go unregistered. Sensitive quartz crystals inside glistening microphone shells vibrated to the sound of his footsteps, his soft breathing, sending feeble currents along wires—to dead amplifying circuits.

"What is it, Ethel?" Dr. Victor Glassman said to his wife.

"Don't you realize it's almost an hour past your lunch time?" she chided. "Why do you come in here anyway? The Brain was completed six months ago. It won't run away— and it won't come to life until someone finds the proper chemical for the nerve fluid to make it work. My goodness. Eight hundred and fifty million dollars sitting idle in here. It gives me gooseflesh. Now you come and eat your lunch so I can get the dishes out of the way. I'm going to be busy the rest of the afternoon getting ready for the crowd—or did you forget that your ten scientists are invited to dinner this evening?"

"Of course not, Ethel," he said, putting his arm around her waist. He pulled her around so they were side by side, looking upward into the maze of catwalks, seeing the marble panels of the wall that served as a covering for the huge man-made brain. *"You* know why I come in here," he said. "I like the feel. The sleeping giant. Not sleeping, really. Just not born yet. Not living yet. Someday soon that will change. The first non-human…"

"I understand, Victor," Ethel said softly. "It scares me. I know it will be just like a human mind—same principles of thought—even if it will be housed in so vast a brain. But how much do we know of the capabilities of the *human* brain? I'm afraid."

Dr. Glassman's eyes crinkled good-naturedly. He tightened his arm around her waist.

"I'll protect you, Ethel," he said.

She looked up at the giant structure that dwarfed them to insignificance. "Against that?" she snorted. "What with? A lance and prancing nag of leather and bones like Don Quixote of old?" She slipped her arm around his shoulders, her expression softening. "But I know what you mean. Only…it's…"

"And I know what you mean, too. Sometimes even I'm afraid of it. But once we activate it, it will take years for it to build up a self-integrated mind even equal to a child's. And we'll both be long dead before its intelligence starts climbing above that of man. You know, I'm hungry."

Together, arm in arm, they departed, closing the door. And once again the echoes died away, leaving only the silence.

And the Brain.

CHAPTER TWO

"HOW about being quiet for a minute so I won't get these mixed up?" Earl Frye said, a mask of tolerant good nature concealing his irritation. "By the way, what's wrong with p.n.9? Bottleneck?"

Irene Conner clapped her hand over her mouth and spoke from between her fingers. "Go ahead and pour," she mumbled. "I'll keep quiet for five minutes."

"Okay," Earl said, unaffected by the twinkle in Irene's clear blue eyes, the smooth wave of her blonde hair, the quiet unscientific curves under her lab apron.

He picked the first vial off the tray, read the number on its label and carefully jotted it down on the lab card. He emptied the vial into the small opening on top the pump and flicked the toggle switch. With a smooth whir the pump started. The pressure gauge needle broke from zero and started upward, finally hovering near the seven-ton-per-square-inch mark. He watched as the fluid he had poured emerged into glass tubing no thicker than a human hair, and, under the tons-per-square-inch pressure, stretched into fine fluid columns less than half a dozen molecules thick.

He repeated the performance with another vial and another pump, and another, until all ten pumps were working. He went back to the first one. The fluid had reached the slightly enlarged bubble several inches up the thread-like glass tubes. He shut off the pump, then went through the same routine with the other ten.

"That show I want to see is on at the Rialto, Earl," Irene said. "Just tonight and tomorrow night."

"Good," Earl grunted, starting to recheck the charts. "Let me know if you liked it. If it's any good I might go see it."

"Why don't you come see it with me?" Irene said.

"Uh…" Earl hesitated, not looking up from a chart he was studying.

He was saved by the hall door opening.

"Hi, Basil," he said, taking in Basil Nelson's expression of mild haste, and the empty test tube in his hand.

Irene frowned in annoyance.

Basil looked at her with a mixture of apology and hopefulness, then turned to Earl. "Uh, I came in to borrow some base formula," he said. "Just need a few cc's and didn't want to take the time to get a full gallon from the storeroom."

"Help yourself," Earl said. He grinned sidewise at Irene. "By the way, Irene is looking for someone to go with her to see some show that's on at the Rialto."

"I'll be glad to," Basil said eagerly.

"No thanks," Irene said. "I'm going with my aunt."

"Your aunt?" Basil said. "I didn't know you had an aunt living in Crestmont." He went to a supply shelf over a wall bench and poured some base formula from a rubber tube dangling from a large bottle.

"She just arrived in town," Irene said dryly.

"Can I meet her?" Basil said coming back from the supply shelf. He was facing Irene and half-facing Earl. He was in a position so that there was nothing between him and the window across the room.

"Sorry," Irene said. "She's leaving town in the morning. I'm sure— Oh, how can you be so clumsy, Basil?"

THE test tube had dropped from his hand. Small glass fragments and the oily fluid were spattered on the floor and his shoes. He was examining a small cut on the inside of his thumb that was beginning to bleed.

"Clumsy?" He said absently. "Oh no. I didn't drop the test tube. It broke in my hand."

"It couldn't have," Irene said accusingly. "You dropped it."

"What's the difference?" Earl said. "Here. I'll get you another test tube with some base fluid. No harm done."

He opened a drawer and took out a new test tube. When he was closing the drawer he glanced absently toward the window. His eyes widened. "What the devil!" he exclaimed. "Look at that. The window's broken too."

"That's odd—too strange a coincidence," Basil frowned.

"Supersonic vibrations?" Earl said, smiling. "Maybe a foreign spy has heard of Project Synthetic Nerve Fluid and was trying to kill Basil with a new secret weapon!"

"Ha ha," Basil said without humor. He accepted the test tube of base formula from Earl. "Thanks, Earl," he said. He went to the door. There he turned appealingly to Irene. "I would like to take you—and your aunt—to the show, Irene," he said.

"Sorry," Irene said, smiling at him sympathetically. "We'll have too much we want to talk about."

"Uh—okay," Basil said unhappily.

"He's such a jerk," Irene said when Basil had left. "All he would do is fawn over me all evening. I'd—I'd rather go alone," she added, looking at Earl appealingly.

"Sure," Earl said. "Be sure and let me know how you like the show. Now—" He smiled half jokingly to take the sting from his words. "Scram. I've got work to do."

Irene made a face at him and went to the door.

When she was gone, Earl sighed wearily. Then he frowned at the broken window.

Carefully he stood where Basil had been standing when the test tube broke. He held his hand in approximately the same position that Basil had held it. Trying not to move his hand, he stooped and squinted over his hand toward the broken window, and beyond it.

A hundred yards away, outside the room, a small hill rose above the wall surrounding the research building. Earl fixed a spot and then went to the window to examine it more closely.

Uneasily he stood so that he was half concealed by the wall of the room. He studied the hill for a minute.

He went to a door at the far side of his lab, and went through into a large room where he had his living quarters. He took some keys from his pocket as he approached a desk. He unlocked the top right hand drawer and took out a small blunt automatic. He checked it and put it in his hip pocket. He slipped off his lab apron and put on a suit coat.

A few minutes later he was approaching the spot he had picked out on the side of the hill. There were trees and shrubs that hid the ground. He watched worriedly, the automatic in his hand now. But there seemed nothing to be alarmed about. Nothing could be more peaceful than the wooded hillside. And yet whatever had caused the simultaneous breaking of the windowpane and the test tube could not have been caused by natural means.

Something, directly ahead, concealed by shrubs, had caused it. What? He intended to find out.

He circled to the left, walking cautiously. With his left hand he parted branches to see into a thicket.

Almost at once he saw the strange structure. It was shaped like a puffball, three feet in diameter at its thickest part, and almost as high. Its surface was of something that had an oily blue sheen. Its base seemed partly buried in the soil, and the ground was freshly damaged as though the ball-like shape had landed with great force.

To add to the evidence that it had fallen from great height, the side was split open and dozens of small semi-transparent balls of different colors were spilled out onto the grass and weeds.

He pushed aside the bushes and approached, slowly putting the automatic back in his hip pocket. He stooped and picked up one of the small colored balls. It was a semi-transparent green.

He put the small ball in his coat pocket. He stooped and examined the break in the wall of the structure. The break faced toward the windows of his lab. He looked in that direction, and saw that leaves obscuring his view were shredded as though by a violent wind.

He found a fragment of the broken wall of the structure, a piece that was hardly more than a sliver. He put that in his shirt pocket. Then, with sudden decision, he scooped up dozens of the marble-like colored balls and loaded his pockets.

BACK in his lab again, he emptied the balls from his pockets into two measuring flasks on a bench. They were strangely light, and one or two had to be put back in the flasks again after they floated slowly upward and down to the table surface where they rested without bouncing.

Earl was filled with excitement and eagerness. This was something entirely outside his experience, something with mystery. It occurred to him that the strange structure might be a new type of bomb. Certainly all the evidence indicated it had dropped from a great height. He dismissed the possible danger with a shrug. He considered the possibility of it being some form of puffball that had sprung up in the shaded woods. It was a remote possibility.

He took the small fragment of the shell from his shirt pocket and stepped to the bench where his microscope stood. If it was living substance it would have cellular structure.

Using the low power objective lens he examined the fragment. It showed no signs of cellular structure. Instead, it was semi-crystalline, similar to a plastic, under the low power lens.

A sharp sound behind him made him straighten and whirl around, his hand going toward the gun that was still in his hip pocket. His hand froze on the butt of the gun. He could only stare.

On the table where he had placed the two measuring flasks with the small colored balls, there were two people. A man and a girl. They were perfectly proportioned—and no more than four inches high.

They seemed unaware of his presence. One of the measuring flasks was tipped over—the sound that had attracted his attention. The colored balls were spilled over the table surface. The miniature man was trying to catch one of the balls, which seemed to float weightless like a bubble. On the miniature man's face was an expression of worried concern.

The miniature girl was sitting down as though she had half risen from where she had fallen. She too was reaching for one of the floating balls.

This much Earl saw in that first startled, incredible instant, then details began to filter into his awareness. The man was green. The girl was blue. They were entirely nude, and the color of their skin was uniform—of the same pastel softness as the colored spheres!

And the girl—Earl found his eyes drawn toward her almost to the exclusion of everything else. She was beautiful beyond anything he had ever imagined.

Her smile was calm, slightly amused, more than a little satisfied and content at some inner thought.

Without thinking, Earl shouted and leaped toward them. His hand descended to catch them. The miniature man looked up at him, startled, then in a desperate attempt to escape leaped over the edge of the table.

The girl had no time to do more than attempt to rise before Earl's fingers closed around her, imprisoning her. He lifted her so that he could see her face more clearly. She stared at him, at first with unmasked terror, then with slowly emerging perplexity and interest.

He became acutely aware of her contours against his hand. What should he do with her? He remembered the man. He would have to catch the man, too!

He looked around on the floor and saw the man peering at him from behind a table leg.

Something would have to be done with the girl. He ran to the door of his room and slipped inside. The windows were closed. She was certainly too small to lift them and escape.

He looked around swiftly, then went to a bookcase and placed her gently on the top shelf.

"Stay there," he warned. He left the room, closing and locking the door.

ACROSS the laboratory he saw the miniature green-skinned man leap to the windowsill below the broken pane. The little man looked over his shoulder and saw Earl. With a desperate leap he reached the jagged edge of glass still in place, and pulled himself through.

Earl rushed to the window in time to see the little man disappear in the high grass growing in the untended grounds outside the building.

Who were these two miniature people? Where had they come from? Had they come in through the broken window in an attempt to steal the colored balls? Were they—*were they from that strange thing out on the side of the hill?* The questions burned through Earl's excited thoughts, demanding answers that wouldn't come.

Those almost weightless balls—Earl crossed to the bench and gathered them up and locked them in a metal drawer.

Nervously, he took out a cigarette and lit it, inhaling deeply. There was the girl, but he found himself reluctant to go in and face her. And yet he had to.

He started toward the hall door, then remembered the gun in his hip pocket. He hesitated, then unlocked the drawer containing the colored balls and placed it in there, locking the drawer again.

He went to the door of his living quarters and unlocked it.

He opened the door a scant inch, took a deep breath, then pushed rapidly, jumped inside, and closed the door at his back so the girl wouldn't have time to escape.

She wasn't blue any more. Her skin was fairly tanned, flawless. But more startling, she was not four inches high. She was, he guessed, five feet two or three. She was the same girl. There was no doubt of that. Her face was the same face, now normal sized. She was the same all over.

"Sorry," Earl gasped. He crossed quickly to his dresser, opened the third drawer and found a pair of pajamas.

"Here," he said, holding them out behind him. "Put these on."

He felt them taken from his hand. A moment later he heard her say, "All right." It was her voice. He listened to it as it echoed in his mind, flavored it. Actually it wasn't anything so wonderful, but it was nice. Nothing seductive or elfin—but she wasn't miniature any more, either. She sounded a little—amused!

He turned to face her.

"I'm Nadine Holmes," the girl said.

"Nadine. That's nice. Holmes...I'm Earl Frye, up until a few minutes ago a quiet research scientist who stays in his lab practically twenty-four hours a day. Nadine Holmes. Were you really small a few minutes ago—or did I imagine it?"

"Yes. I was small... So *you* are Dr. Earl Frye..."

"Yes. But how can you know me?" Earl asked, surprised at her tone. A distant knocking sounded. He groaned. "That's probably Irene," he said. "She'll pound the door down. You stay here and be quiet while I get rid of her. She could cause both of us a lot of trouble."

He went to the door, slipped out, and carefully locked it. The knocking was peremptory at the lab door. "Just a minute," he said. He unlocked the door, prepared to tell Irene she was interrupting some important work. It wasn't Irene. "Oh, it's you, Mrs. Glassman. I didn't know. I was busy and didn't want to be interrupt—that is, come on in." He opened the door invitingly, and glanced worriedly at the door to his living quarters. Had he locked it? Of course he had. He distinctly remembered locking it.

"I'm sorry I interrupted your work," Mrs. Glassman said. "I met Irene—Dr. Connor, you know. She told me you might need some reminding about dinner—seven thirty. I do hope you'll be there."

"I may not have my work done," Earl said weakly.

"Nonsense! It can wait. It will do you good to get away from the lab for an evening. If you aren't there I'll come and get you."

"Okay," Earl said hastily. "I promise to be there—on time."

He locked the hall door after Mrs. Glassman.

HE glanced thoughtfully at the pump bench with its ten sets of glass threads containing ten different fluids, ready for cutting and connecting to the test instruments for measurement of speed and sustainment of molecular chain action.

The theory of what he was looking for—what all ten of the scientists were looking for in their planned exploration of a few dozen thousand substances, was fairly simple. The molecule in theory had to be of a special type, of which there were many examples. It had to consist of two parts; one larger than the other, such that the smaller part could break off easily and jump to the next molecule, combining with it and freeing its counterpart on that next molecule, so that the freed part would repeat the performance on the next, and so on. In that way, the ion of the lesser molecular part, starting at one end of the chain of identical molecules, would start a chain of reactions, which would end in an identical free ion at the farther end of the glass thread. In effect it would be the same as though the free ion had passed quickly through the full length of the fine tube—without any of the molecules actually having moved at all.

Unfortunately, so far, none of the substances tried had behaved quite as they should in theory. It was impossible to get a tube fine enough for a thread one molecule thick, with the molecules lined up properly.

With some of the test substances the "nerve impulse" would go part way and then turn around and come back. With others it would just "get lost." Super-delicate instruments "followed" the impulse, telling what happened to it in fine detail.

Nerve fluid from living animals had been tested and found to behave properly even in the fine glass tubing. But it was highly unstable. If a synthetic brain capable of integrated thought processes was to be constructed, a non-deteriorating nerve fluid would have to be found. One that duplicated the performance of the actual nerve threads of the human brain.

All that held back Project Brain was the proper synthetic nerve fluid. Maybe it's one of those ten, Earl thought. But he entertained that thought with every ten he tested.

But right now there was a more pressing problem. Nadine Holmes. She should have arrived on the afternoon bus—instead of appearing as a pastel blue miniature girl on a bench in his lab—and growing to an embarrassing full five foot three of emotion disturbing nudity in a few minutes. An impossible fact, but still a fact.

Where had she come from? That was what he had been going to ask her when Ethel Glassman barged in. Dear old Mrs. Glassman.

CHAPTER THREE

EARL went to the door to his living quarters and unlocked it. Slipping in quickly, he locked the door again. Nadine was curled up in a chair, one of his technical books on her lap, looking altogether too domestic for Earl's peace of mind. She had paused in her reading, and was looking up at him questioningly.

"Now then," Earl said. He groped for a sequence of thought. She was beautiful. "Now then," he repeated. "We've got to get you some decent clothes and decide what to do with you. What sizes do you wear?"

"I don't know," Nadine said. "I've never worn clothes before. I don't think I like them."

"You'll get used to them," Earl said hastily. "Those things you have on are my pajamas. We'll need some nylon stockings, shoes, and other things. I'll have to go buy them."

"Do you have other clothes like the ones you are wearing?" Nadine asked. "Why wouldn't they do? They're too large, but I could wear them."

Earl stared at her in amazement. And now the big question came again. He moved closer to her. "Where do you come from?"

She puzzled over his words. "I'm not sure what you're talking about," she said, a tone of wariness in her voice. "Where I come from—perhaps we'd better not discuss that now. I don't quite understand what happened. Things didn't happen as they were supposed to. Could you take me where you first found me?"

"Not until I get you some clothes. Imagine what people would think if you walked out of here wearing my pajamas!"

"What would they think?" Nadine said, frankly puzzled. "Why are clothes? Are they connected in some way with religion? I think that's the word for it—religion. Do clothes bring you good luck? Is that it? You seem so—so intense about it. Does everyone wear them?"

He ignored her question, went out, locking the door. Before he opened the lab door to the hall he glanced at his watch. An hour ago nothing had happened. He shook his head, opened the door and stepped into the hall—almost bumping into Basil Nelson.

"Hi, Earl," Basil said. "You look like you're in a hurry."

"I am," Earl said. He started past Basil, who fell into step beside him.

"I'll go along," Basil said. "That is, if you don't mind. I wanted to talk with you. Pretty important. It's about Irene."

"What about Irene?" Earl said.

Basil waited until they were on the sidewalk before answering. "I guess it's pretty obvious I'm in love with her," he said. "But—she seems to have eyes only for you. Mrs. Glassman sort of hinted that you and Irene—well—were going to get married. I wanted to ask you. If you and Irene are—"

"*Damn* Ethel Glassman," Earl said, irritated. "If you are in love with her why don't you tell her?"

"She won't give me the chance to tell her," Basil groaned. "I think she suspects, though," he added darkly.

"Fine," Earl said. "And there's no time like the present. Why don't you go back and pop the question right now while you have your nerve up?"

Basil sighed. "I'll have to work up to it. Right now I'd rather tag along with you. Mind?"

"No," Earl groaned. "Not at all. A—cousin of mine has a birthday coming up. I thought I'd buy her some new clothes. No use you tagging along."

"Don't mind at all," Basil said. "We can do some more talking. Maybe we could cook up some scheme to make Irene fall in love with me. But every time I think I'm going great with her I pull something like dropping that test tube in your lab."

"Oh, that," Earl said. "I—" He clamped his lips shut.

"SEE you at Glassman's at dinner tonight," Earl said firmly an hour later. As Basil still hesitated, he added, "Maybe I can think of something by then. Meanwhile I've still got work to do."

"Uh, oh sure," Basil said, "but I'm afraid it's no use. She's in love with you, Earl."

"Nonsense!" Earl unlocked the door to his lab and went in with his packages. He stacked them on a lab table and locked the hall door. A quick survey showed the lab as it should be. Earl had been worried. Since Nadine had become a full sized person, maybe the little green man had, too…

Earl crossed to the door to his living quarters and unlocked it. Inside, he saw Nadine still curled up in the chair in his pajamas, a stack of books beside her.

"Hi," Earl said, subdued. "I've brought you some clothes, and also some literature on what they are. I think the literature will give you enough data to work on in dressing."

He brought the stack of packages into the room and put them on a table.

"While you're dressing I'll finish some work out in the lab," he said.

"Clothes seem terribly important to you," Nadine said without moving from her comfortable position. "I still can't understand why. I've tried and tried." She picked up a book. "This book, for example. It's a very vivid account of a murder. I can understand vaguely about the murder. It seems to be some sort of game that people play. There are official players who earn their living at it. The taxpayers pay them for it, and they sit in their offices until some taxpayer wants to play with them. The taxpayer kills someone. The detectives must find out who he is if they can. I can understand that. But there are whole passages where everyone seems to forget the game while they pay great attention to what someone is wearing. That's it! It must be another game. No?"

Earl grinned. "That's pretty close," he said. "Do you have games where you come from?"

"No. Games aren't functional."

"Oh," Earl said vaguely. "Well, get those clothes on, Nadine. You will look terrific in them."

He backed out of the room and closed the door. While he worked he wondered how Nadine could speak English without an accent. It was too far-fetched to think it her native language. Even if it were, spoken language changes so rapidly that the only possible explanations were, (1) she was from some part of the United States, or (2), her people were in constant radio contact with current broadcasts. But neither alternative could account for her inability to grasp the purpose of clothes. He hadn't had quite enough nerve to mention to her the main purpose—sex. Maybe she had been too shy to mention it too. But that didn't seem to jibe with her evident willingness to take off her clothes. And she hadn't answered his question on where she came from.

WHILE Earl thought these thoughts he let his hands and one part of his mind put the synthetic nerve filaments in place in the instrument banks. There wouldn't be time to run the tests, but he could do that in the morning when he was alone.

Alone. The thought struck him with dismaying force. He realized suddenly that he had been trying to keep Nadine with him as long as possible—and that was futile.

Was he in love with her? He faced the question squarely and felt his stomach turn over and his heart start to pound wildly. He tried to tell himself it was just the unusualness of the situation.

He was jerked out of his thoughts by the sound of high-heeled shoes. Nadine had opened the door and taken a few steps into the lab. His eyes approved of what they saw.

"They're very uncomfortable," Nadine said. "Especially the shoes. But I looked at myself in the mirror—and I think I begin to understand, a little. Clothes are adornments."

"On you they are," Earl said. "I never before realized…"

"What's a kiss?" Nadine said.

Earl blinked. He cleared his throat loudly and said, "One thing at a time, Nadine. There's lots for you to learn. In the meantime, how does it happen you know English so well? If you're from—some other planet—you certainly don't speak it as your native language."

"It was taught to us for the expedition," Nadine said. "I think there must have been an accident. Can you tell me anything about it? The first I remember is just before you picked me up in your enormous hand."

Earl told her everything he knew. She listened, nodding her head at times.

"I think I understand now," she said when he finished. "The stasis spheres. Somehow mine and George Ladd's were fractured, so that we emerged on the bench. He was in the green one."

"You mean you were *in* one of those marbles?" Earl exclaimed.

"Where is the ship?" Nadine said.

Earl took her to the window and pointed out the spot. "You can't see it from here," he said. "But I have some of the—what did you call them? Stasis spheres? I'll show you."

He unlocked the drawer. Nadine leaned over, seeming to look inside of each translucent marble.

"Yes," she said, straightening. "It's gone wrong, somehow. The Cyberene will be most annoyed."

"The Cyberene? What's that?"

Nadine stared down into the drawer, frowning. "You wouldn't understand," she said. And then, "I'm hungry."

Earl frowned. "That reminds me. I have to go to dinner at Dr. Glassman's in a little while, or Mrs. Glassman will come barging in here. I'll fix you something first. After I get back I'll take you to a hotel."

Nadine perched on the edge of the table in his kitchenette while he opened some cans and heated their contents.

"How does it smell?" Earl asked after a while. "Good?"

"Strange," Nadine said. "Not entirely strange. Some of the smells are familiar."

"Would you like a cocktail?" Earl said. He didn't wait for her answer. He was acutely conscious of playing the host. "This is my favorite drink. A dash of rum, a little vodka, lime juice, powdered sugar, ice cubes and seltzer. There." He handed her one of the two glasses. "How do you like it?"

Nadine sipped the drink cautiously. "Good," she said. "I was thirsty too."

"What is the Cyberene?" Earl said, dishing steaming food into a plate set precariously on the edge of the stove.

"The—the Cyberene," Nadine said as though that explained it. "How do you eat that food without getting dirty? And there's such an enormous amount of it. I'm used to capsules, with lots of water to help digest them."

"Oh. Dehydrated foods," Earl said. "Damn, I wish I didn't have to go to that dinner. Stay in here while I change my clothes."

"Earl," Nadine said as he was about to leave the room.

"Yes?" he said, turning to look at her questioningly.

"What does damn mean? I can't get the sense of it."

"It's an adornment of speech," he said. "Like clothes."

WITH dinner over, Earl drifted toward the door after excusing himself and thanking the Glassmans. Basil followed him.

"I need someone to talk to—to help me, Basil," Earl said as they walked back toward the lab building. "Remember that test tube breaking? And the window pane?"

"How can I forget?" Basil said ruefully.

Quickly Earl outlined everything that had happened.

"What you should have done," Basil said in amazement, "is gone directly to Dr. Glassman with it. Now nobody will believe you. Even I find it hard to believe. You must have fallen hard, the way you want to keep her under lock and key."

"It's not that," Earl said. "Just a lot of little things. Like her repeating my name as if she knew all about me. And her refusing to say where she's from. And her knowledge of our language yet knowing absolutely nothing about our social customs."

"What about time travel?" Basil said.

"Time travel? That's absurd."

"Why?"

"If time travel were possible at any future date, we would have time travelers all around us. They'd come back."

"Maybe they have," Basil said darkly. "What did she call those colored marbles you found? Stasis spheres? But the main thing right now is that if I were in this George Ladd's shoes—"

"He doesn't wear shoes."

"Well, I would be trying to rescue Nadine Holmes this very minute. It's dark now—"

But Earl wasn't listening. Basil hurried to catch up with him as he walked rapidly, until they reached the lab building resting against the giant starless bulk of the dome that housed the Brain.

"Be quiet," Earl warned as they stole down the hall toward the door to his lab.

They reached the door and stopped. Through the panel came the sound of a male voice, the words indistinguishable but the tones unmistakably demanding and insistent.

Nadine's voice answered, its tones firm. Earl and Basil looked at each other. Neither of those inside were speaking English.

The male voice uttered a harsh monosyllable. Nadine screamed. Earl, abandoning caution, tried to open the door. It was locked. He wasted precious seconds getting the key into the lock. Cursing at the delay, he flung the door open and ran toward the two figures struggling near the windows. One was Nadine, her clothes torn, her face a mask of desperate effort to escape. The other, Earl recognized instantly as being George Ladd. He also recognized the suit Ladd was wearing. It was one of his own.

CHAPTER FOUR

LADD didn't seem to be aware of him until he grabbed him by the shoulder and pulled him around roughly. For a split second George Ladd was motionless with surprise—and in that split second Earl lashed out with his fist.

The blow sent Ladd stumbling backward until he was brought up against a table. Earl leaped toward him. Ladd made no attempt to escape, but fumbled for something in the coat pocket of the suit he was wearing. A glistening object appeared in his hand.

Earl swerved, thinking it must be a gun. Then he was sprawling full length on the floor, his muscles refusing to obey his commands. His consciousness was almost entirely dominated by a terrible tingling sensation that seemed to possess every cell of his body from the neck down.

He had fallen in such a way that he saw Basil leaping forward. The next instant Basil was plunging floorward, his arms refusing to come up to break his fall.

Nadine was running toward the open hall door. She too fell sprawling.

George Ladd appeared in Earl's line of vision. He closed the door and locked it from the inside, then picked Nadine up and cradled her limp body over his shoulder.

Earl tried to cry out. The tingling in his throat became unbearable. In numb horror and frustrated rage he watched George Ladd, Nadine over his shoulder, her arms dangling limply. A moment later he heard a window raised. There were sounds of heavy exertion, a faint thud outside the window. Then silence.

Earl's eyes fell on Basil's motionless form. For what might have been minutes or hours the tingling continued. It died away with imperceptible slowness. Finally he was able to move a little. A minute later he was able to sit up. His entire body felt as though it had "been asleep."

Almost immediately Basil moved. Earl reached out for the nearest table and pulled himself to his feet, fighting to keep his legs from caving.

Basil rose to a sitting position, shook his head to clear his senses, looked up at Earl, and grinned feebly. He said, his speech thick and clumsy, "Now I believe you. That paralysis gun did it."

Earl was startled. "You didn't believe me before?"

"Hell no," Basil sighed. "I just thought you were going a long ways to explain what some people would call a sordid affair." His grin became more natural. "I was right though. This George Ladd is now a hero." He frowned. "Only—your Nadine didn't seem to want to be rescued."

"Get up and move around," Earl said desperately. "Get some circulation back. We may still be able to catch up with them and get her back."

"I don't know," Basil said doubtfully, getting to his feet. "I hate the idea of that paralysis gun."

"I've got a gun, too," Earl said.

He half stumbled toward the bench with the locked drawer. He searched for his keys, remembered he had left them in the hall door. He started for the door, then stopped. The locked drawer was open and damaged. A heavy screwdriver was on the table over it. The drawer was empty.

"He got my gun!" Earl said. "He got the stasis spheres too!"

Basil came to stand beside him and stare broodingly into the empty drawer. "That does it," he mumbled. "Now you don't have anything."

"There's that thing out on the hill," Earl said. "Maybe George Ladd headed for that. He hasn't had time to get located in town. We can find him hiding out there. Wait until I get a flashlight."

From another drawer he brought out a high-powered flashlight. He went to the open window and crawled out. Basil hesitated, then followed him.

BEHIND them was the building they had just left, light streaming from the open window and from half a dozen other windows. To their right loomed the dark bulk of the dome that housed the gigantic Brain, an obsidian shape in the night that hulked into the heavens, blotting out a hemisphere of stars. Ahead, above the horizon, was a crescent moon that served to silhouette the hill and its horizon of trees. Around them were dark shapes motionless.

Earl kept the flashlight ready, but didn't use it as they stole swiftly forward. Neither man spoke, but their breathing was a stentorian sound that blended with distant traffic noises and the nearby chirping of a cricket, and the rustling of weeds as they forced them aside in their passage.

They reached the hill and went forward more slowly, using caution as they remembered the effects of the paralysis gun. Now Earl was remembering the way he had come before finding landmarks in the darkness. At last he stopped and touched Basil's arm to bring him to a halt.

"It's on the other side of these bushes," he whispered. "I'll use the flash."

He parted the branches. Suddenly a cone of light exploded in the darkness.

"Right there," Basil said. Then, in surprise, "It's gone!"

"Naturally," Earl said in some disgust. "It fits the pattern."

"What pattern?" Basil asked.

Earl was slow in answering. He said, "I don't know. I just felt it. Or maybe I do know. Nadine and that guy Ladd were small and got big in a hurry. What was to keep that thing from doing the same? That's part of it. The other part is just a feeling. They don't seem to want to advertise to the world that they're here. Maybe the damn thing became invisible or something. With stasis spheres and small people that get big, and paralysis guns, what's so impossible about that ship or whatever it is getting big and becoming invisible? I'll bet it's still there."

But though they passed back and forth over the entire area, with increasing boldness, they encountered nothing, visible or invisible, that was out of the ordinary.

There was a concave depression in the soil where Earl remembered the puffball shape to have been. Even fresh scars in the dirt around the depression.

For a while Earl blundered through the underbrush calling Nadine's name cautiously, without hope. Finally they were forced to give up and return to the lab building.

"We could call the police," Basil said doubtfully.

"Oh, sure," Earl said, his voice harsh. "What would we tell them? Dr. Glassman would be called in. Next they'd call the boys in the white jackets."

"Maybe they're just the boys we need," Basil said. "Or a good stiff drink. I like the idea of the drink."

IT was ten o'clock in the morning when Irene Conner pushed open the door without knocking and strolled casually into Earl's laboratory. She saw him at the far end of the room, hunched over with his elbows on the windowsill, his back to her.

"Hi, Earl," she called cheerfully. "Want to have mid-morning coffee with me?"

"No," Earl said without moving.

"You sound tired," Irene said going over to stand beside him. "Or is it spring fever—more accurately the summer doldrums."

"Neither," he said, glancing up at her with tired eyes. "I just want to be left alone. I'm thinking." He straightened up with a deep sigh. "Why don't you get Basil to have coffee with you?"

"That jerk?" Irene said. "He gets in my hair."

"Like you get in mine?" Earl said.

"That was cruel."

"Sorry," Earl relented. "I didn't get much sleep last night. I've got problems. I'd much rather be left alone with them right now."

Irene inspected him critically as a man might inspect his automobile. "Your eyes are bloodshot," she said. "Why not have some coffee with me and tell me your problems. Maybe I can help you."

"Nobody can help me—least of all you."

The phone on the desk in the corner rang. Earl went to answer it.

"This is Glassman," the phone said. "I want a general staff meeting in my office at once. Tell Dr. Conner she must be there, too."

"Okay," Earl said. He hung up and looked at Irene. "Goat face," he explained. "General staff meeting. We're to go to his office at once."

"Maybe this is it," Irene said, suddenly sober.

Earl nodded. That was the way it would come. A phone call for general staff meeting. A quiet announcement that one of the scientists had at last found the ideal nerve fluid for the brain. That's all there would be to it. The greatest achievement since—if not including—the atom bomb, and the historic moment would pass without a shout—with perhaps only a tired sigh of relief, a glance of envy at the lucky one who had found it.

"Well, let's get it over with," Earl said.

They went into the hall and walked side by side in silence toward the back of the building where it joined the Dome. Basil joined them, for once hardly noticing Irene as he looked questioningly at Earl, who shook his head imperceptibly.

They entered Dr. Glassman's office. The director was sitting behind his desk, ignoring them, pretending to be reading some typewritten papers.

Earl looked around. They were all there now, he and the other nine scientists, and Dr. Glassman. Only there was something wrong with the picture . One of them should have been beaming at the others, the light of triumph in his or her eyes. Instead, the other nine reflected his own puzzled bewilderment.

"Sit down, sit down," Dr. Glassman said, looking up at them. He waited until they were all seated about the room, then cleared his throat importantly, pushing aside the papers he had been reading. He started to say something, then became aware of their expressions. He shook his head. "The end isn't in sight yet. But we may be closer than we think. I'll introduce you in a moment to a new addition to our staff. A person who—from the reports I've seen from Washington—seems to be quite a genius at creating new type molecules, tailor-made for specific tasks. Our new associate won't be assigned a separate lab. Instead, will serve as a sort of general consultant, observing all your work, and will make suggestions for hastening things up a bit." A murmur of voices and sharp footsteps came from the hall. "My wife has been showing our new colleague the Brain. I think they're coming now."

The door opened. Mrs. Glassman's cheerful face appeared. "They're all here now," she said over her shoulder.

The door opened farther. Earl, and everyone else, was staring at the opening, waiting for their first glimpse of the newcomer.

Earl half rose to his feet before he stopped himself. Then he slowly sat down, his eyes wide and puzzled.

IT was Nadine. She wasn't wearing the clothes he had bought for her the day before. Instead, she was dressed in a stylishly cut business suit and low-heeled slippers, a trim hat covering her hair. She had paused just inside the room, a half smile on her carefully painted lips. Her eyes surveyed each face pleasantly, passing over Earl's as though she had never seen him before.

"Come up here, my dear," Dr. Glassman said in honeyed tones. And to the others, "I want you to meet Dr. Nadine Holmes." Then back to her, "What did you think of the Brain? Quite an imposing thing, isn't it?"

"Yes, it is," Nadine replied. "I felt quite—awed by it, sitting there where it will remain for untold centuries, waiting only for the vital fluid that will give it the ability to think."

"I'm sure it won't be untold centuries before it gets the fluid," Dr. Glassman said, chuckling heartily at his own humor. "I'll introduce you to your co-workers, Dr. Holmes. This is Dr. Paul Hardwick…"

Earl caught Basil's attention and shook his head warningly. He waited, then, for his turn at being introduced, his heart pounding violently, his pulse racing.

"…and this is Dr. Earl Frye…" Dr. Glassman said.

"How do you do, Dr. Frye." Nadine's hand was smooth and cool as she rested it in his. Her eyes sized him up with impersonal interest, but without a flicker of recognition.

"…and this is Dr. Basil Nelson…"

Nadine withdrew her hand gently and moved on.

"And now you may return to your work," Dr. Glassman announced. "I know the male members of the staff will be waiting for a visit from our charming new member, but you must be patient. She will get around to all of you in the next few days."

Earl was in the hall before Glassman had finished. He wanted to think. Rapid footsteps caught up with him. "*Now* can we have coffee?" she asked with humorous petulance.

"No!" Earl said with more fierceness in his voice than he had intended. It had the effect of a physical blow on Irene. She fell back a step, blinking.

Basil caught up with them. "I want to talk with you, Earl," he said.

"Basil," Irene cut in, "will *you* have coffee with me?"

"Me?" Basil said in delight. "Sure." He linked his arm in hers. "Let's go." He looked back over his shoulder at Earl. "Thanks, Earl," he said. "I'll see you later." It was two hours later...

CHAPTER FIVE

"YOU sure it's her?" Basil said. "I'm inclined to agree with you. Of course, I saw her only for a second or two... Where do you suppose she picked up those snazzy clothes? I was watching her when she was introduced to you. Boy, is she some actress!"

"I'm wondering if it was an act," Earl said frowning.

"Of course it was—had to be if she's the same girl. But she didn't let on she knew you at all."

"That's why I wonder if it was an act. There was something strange about her. I can't quite put my finger on it—or yes I can. She's changed. Today her whole personality is different. And where did she get papers authentic enough to fool Glassman?"

"Why don't you ask her when she comes here?" Basil suggested.

Earl shook his head. "I wonder if she could be under some sort of hypnosis? No, wait. It isn't any more absurd than a paralysis gun. If she doesn't stay here tonight I'm going to follow her and see where she goes. Are you with me?"

"Uh…" Basil hesitated. "Depends on when she leaves the building. Irene and I have sort of a date to have dinner at the Red Barn at six o'clock."

"Go ahead," Earl said, grinning. "I'll probably have more success alone anyway. We'd get in each other's way."

"Why don't you ask Glassman where she's staying? It's probably some hotel in town."

"I'll think about it," Earl said. When Basil left, Earl went to the window and looked toward the hill. Would Nadine go there? Was there some hiding place on the hill where she would go, to wait until tomorrow, after her "day's work" was done?

Earl nodded to himself. It had to be. Nothing else fitted into the crazy pattern of events.

One thing he was certain of now. In spite of the accident that had broken open the "ship" when it landed out there, its coming here—or here and now—was no accident. Nor Nadine's apparent familiarity with his name the night before, or her showing up now with credentials that gave her the run of the place in an almost supervisory capacity.

And that meant that her interest was in the Brain. Hers— and who else? George Ladd, of course. How many more? If each of those stasis spheres had contained a person, there were dozens more in on it.

Then why had Nadine been sent into the open when she was certain to be recognized by him?

That was what had been bothering him from the instant she walked into Glassman's office. On the surface it was the most stupid thing that could have occurred. On the surface...

Stupid. Yet somehow stupid didn't seem to fit. Maybe it had been exceedingly cunning. Maybe there was something he had missed.

Cunning it might be—or stupid. But there was something else about it that neither adjective quite fit. There was obviously organization in back of Nadine. People. A "ship". Paralysis guns and what they implied. Therefore planning, colored by one accident. Suppose every detail of the plan had been worked out ahead of time, and was going ahead without alteration. Suppose the original plan had specified that Nadine was to be the "front", and the plan was proceeding blindly, on the behavior level of instinct in animals who repeat instinctive routines made senseless by changed environment. Or the blind function level of a machine that keeps turning out parts when the conveyor belt has stopped; until it wrecks itself...

It annoyed Earl not to be able to pin his thoughts down, to bring everything into full focus.

HE went to his kitchenette and fixed a hasty lunch. All afternoon he worked, immersed in the routine of testing chemicals in batches of ten and making out report sheets on each one. And all afternoon he puzzled over what could be behind Nadine's having shown up. Not so much what might be behind her having returned to the scene, nor her not recognizing him, but *why* someone else hadn't been used.

No one dropped in. Irene's absence gave him only a sense of relief. Basil, no doubt, was staving away because of a guilt complex. Nadine—her continued absence could be because she wasn't ready for him yet, or she truly didn't remember him and would get to him in due time, perhaps tomorrow; or maybe the Plan involved some other member of the research group. Or the destruction of the Brain? Earl shook his head at this thought. That alternative didn't fit.

And then it was four-thirty. Already Earl had reasoned out what he intended to do. Either Nadine would go into town and stay at a hotel, remain in the building as a guest of the Glassmans', or she would leave the building and make her way by some circuitous route to the spot on the hill where the "ship" had been.

Only the latter possibility interested Earl right now. He quickly slipped off his lab apron and put on a suit coat. He wished that he still had a gun, but it had been stolen with the stasis spheres. He'd have to do without it.

Leaving the building, he walked along the sidewalk until he was able to approach the hill from the other side where he wouldn't be seen from the windows.

It was ten minutes to five when he settled down to wait in the concealment of a thicket where he could command a view of the approaches from every direction, and a clear view of the slight depression in the ground where the "ship" had dropped.

There was nothing to do now but wait—and stay awake. He was acutely aware, suddenly, of his lack of sleep the night before. A warm breeze rustled the leaves around him. A small hop toad paused to stare up at him in unblinking fixity.

Overhead in a large Maple tree a host of sparrows paused to hold a brief political convention.

And then Nadine was coming up the slope from the side away from the lab. Her chic hat dangled carelessly in her right hand, the warm breeze mussing her hair. A too normal smart-looking woman's purse was under her arm. The breeze caught her skirt, molding her graceful legs, her slim body.

She was too much the picture of a normal girl idly strolling in a park.

A great nostalgia, an almost overwhelming yearning, took possession of Earl. He wanted to rush forward, let her know he was there, waiting for her.

Instead, he remained motionless, watching her approach.

She seemed to be heading straight for him. For an instant he thought she must have seen him. But her expression held no excitement or anything but half dreamy enjoyment of her surroundings.

SCARCELY fifteen feet away she came to a stop and turned to face toward the concave depression in the ground, another fifty feet beyond her. With her free hand she reached up and patted at her hair like any normal girl would do, unconsciously.

Abruptly Earl became aware of something just beyond her. It wasn't tangible. A shimmering in the air. A slight but definite refractive quality that had not been there the moment before.

Nadine had seen it too. She walked forward a few steps.

"This is it!" Earl thought to himself. He crouched to run after her.

She took another step. She vanished, not abruptly, but as one might vanish into a bright silver but otherwise transparent fog.

In that instant Earl moved, hurtling forward so that when she disappeared he was a step behind her.

Instantly the peaceful wooded scene vanished. His feet were on a smooth hard floor. Ahead of him he caught a brief glimpse of walls, of people without clothes.

Then he was falling over Nadine and trying to keep from falling on her. His arms were around her. Somehow he twisted so that when he landed she was on top, unhurt.

There was a stunned eternity when her eyes were looking into his, recognition and gladness unmasked, hope and pleading sending him some secret message, some unspoken word trembling on her lips.

But Earl had seen George Ladd even as he fell, and the never forgotten instincts developed in him during World War III were in motion, making him continue his roll so that in the next instant he was on his feet, Nadine behind him. Ladd hadn't expected this and was caught by surprise. Earl took advantage of that brief uncertainty, stepping in and bringing a short chopping right against Ladd's jaw.

Before George Ladd reached the floor, Earl was running in great strides, his eyes darting ahead in search of a place to escape.

"Wait!" Nadine called. But he didn't pause. He couldn't trust her. George Ladd had been armed with his paralysis gun. He'd been waiting for him. This had been a trap, and Nadine had led him into it.

Ahead was a doorway. He hesitated. Should he continue on down the corridor or take the doorway? He decided on the latter. It opened into a room, unoccupied at the moment. There were windows. One of them was open. Earl didn't hesitate. Beyond the window was a wide paved street. If he could get away, mingle with crowds…

No one was in sight. He sprinted along the pavement, away from the Dome, which he had glimpsed over his shoulder. It was beautiful, its basic structure adorned with granite superstructures of fine workmanship. But he didn't pause to admire it. He wanted people, lots of people, to mix with and hide from pursuit.

For a hundred yards the street went through parkways. Then ahead were buildings. He reached them, racing along a canyon formed by windowless walls of buildings. He rounded a corner. The street was still deserted.

He ran on and on, turning corners when he came to them, but always heading in one general direction so as not to circle back toward the Dome.

ABRUPTLY he paused. Beside him was a door in a building. He darted inside, closing the door behind him and leaning against it while he breathed in rasping gulps of air.

Ahead of him was a corridor and more doors. After a brief rest he sprinted down the hallway. If he could find a vacant room, a place to hide until he could map out some plan...

He listened at the first door. There was no sound. He tried the knob. The door opened silently under his touch. He stepped in. The room was unoccupied. Its far wall was of glass. He glanced through it. He was looking out over an enormous workshop of some kind. Row upon row of small vats were there—and people.

He was seeing his first people of this world he had plunged into. They wore no clothes. They seemed to be tending the vats, walking along the aisles, pausing here and there at a vat to touch banks of controls and watch what was in each vat.

From the hall Earl had just left came loud voices. The words were in a strange language, but the tones carried their own message. His pursuers had caught up with him. In another moment they would open the door and find him.

He looked around for a way to escape. There was a trap door in the floor. It undoubtedly led to the huge workshop. Earl lifted the door and saw a ladder. He climbed onto it, letting the trap door fall back into place as he descended.

He fully expected workers to see him and react to his presence in some way. A worker was less than ten feet away. The worker didn't pause or seem to notice him.

Silently Earl watched the man's eyes, dull and void of intelligence. They seemed only passive recorders of what there was for him to see. He was touching control knobs in front of a vat.

Earl looked into the vat and caught his breath. Floating in the tank was a human embryo. It was alive, its umbilical cord growing from a spongy mass on the floor of the tank.

Forgetting his danger, Earl grabbed the man's shoulder, "What is this?" he demanded. "Human babies growing in tanks?"

The worker waited unresisting until Earl released his grip, then continued on his routine way. He was, in every respect, a robot, doing his specialized job, his mind a complete blank to anything else. A zombie. Earl looked out over the vast baby factory and realized with numb horror that all the hundreds of people working here were the same. Walking dead, their minds capable of only one thing—doing this specialized task. And the human embryos in the tanks? Would they become walking zombies?

Over his head came the sound of the trap door opening. Earl didn't take time to look up. He ran. Down an aisle between rows of unborn humans tended by undead zombies. Up another ladder into another observation room, ignoring shouts that caught up with him. Out another door, down another hall, through another door, and into a street again.

Miles of streets, and then something recognizable. A factory with belching smokestacks. He plunged toward it recklessly, desperately hoping to find intelligent men. Men with minds. Men able to help him hide.

He found himself inside a huge plant where giant ladles were pouring molten metal into molds. There were men running the machines that controlled the pouring. They wore thick asbestos-like suits.

As Earl ran toward them he saw one of them slip and fall so that his arm went into the stream of molten metal. The man didn't cry out nor jerk away. Splattering metal cascaded on the others. There was the stench of burned flesh.

His mind numb with the shock of what he was seeing, Earl stood rooted, watching the others continue their work with expressionless faces, blank eyes. Mindless creatures, controlled like inanimate robots.

"Earl!"

He turned in the direction of the voice. He saw Nadine beckoning for him to come to her. He started toward her, then stopped. She was different from these—or was she? No, she wasn't any different. She too was an automaton. She was beckoning him to walk into another trap.

He turned to run the other way, but in that moment of indecision he had been surrounded by men like George Ladd, carrying the little paralysis guns—and they were automatons, too.

He turned, searching for a way of escape, the smell of molten-metal and cooked flesh strong in his nostrils. And then he felt the sting of the paralysis gun and was falling forward.

A sharp pain entered the base of his skull. He lost consciousness then with the monstrous horror of what was around him searing into his soul.

THE next instant, it seemed, he awakened, all the horror fresh in his mind, the stinging sensation at the nape of his neck changed to a dull throbbing pain. Nadine had led him into this. But she was like the rest, a zombie unable to think for herself.

He shook his head slowly in pained bewilderment. She hadn't been that way the first time he met her. She had been—*herself*... *What could have created this nightmare?*

A voice somewhere sounded in deep resonant tones. "So you are awake," it said.

Earl rolled onto his side and searched for the source of the voice. There was no one in view. He was in a room whose walls and ceiling were heavy glass. He looked through the ceiling and saw the familiar maze of steel catwalks inside the dome.

Outside his glass prison a pair of video cameras were trained on him. Their lenses seemed somehow sentient, so that their motionlessness partook of the quality of a fixed stare.

"I've always wanted to meet you," the voice said, and it seemed to come from a small case atop the camera frames.

It was a dream, Earl decided. He had been hit on the head. In his delirium he had conjured up the Brain, activated and intelligent as it was designed to be in theory, possessed of a mind of its own.

"Of course," the voice went on, "I've seen film shots of you. You are the discoverer of the nerve fluid that made me possible."

Earl sat up abruptly. "Who are you? And where—"

"I am the *Cyberene*. This is the year 3042 A. D., in the old calendar. I had you brought here through what might be called a time tube from your own period. Shortly you will return through that tube to your own time—as many hours ahead from the time you left as you spend here before you go back."

Earl got to his feet slowly, watching the glistening lenses. "Now it begins to fit together," he said. "You're behind Nadine and Ladd. You say *I'm* the discoverer of the nerve fluid. You're mistaken. It hasn't been found yet—and there are ten of us looking for it. One of the others may be the one to find it."

"History says you found it."

"And you just wanted to see me because of that?" Earl asked.

"Watch," the voice said.

The plate glass wall in front of Earl changed suddenly, to become apparently a giant window overlooking a huge sprawling city. There were buildings that reached thousands of feet into the sky, with fragile looking networks of bridges spanning the spaces among them. There were giant aircraft in the sky. In the distance was a trail of fire that might be from an interplanetary rocket ship departing spaceward.

And abruptly the elfin city was blotted out by a blinding sun. Seconds later the blinding sun was gone, and Earl could see the city again. But now it was only the skeleton of what it had been. Its spiderweb design of bridges was torn and twisted. Many of its tall buildings were even now toppling toward the ground. Fire shot skyward in a pyrotechnic display of havoc.

CHAPTER SIX

A GIANT airplane appeared, heading straight toward the window through which Earl watched. It grew larger. For a brief second he looked into its control cabin and saw its pilot and co-pilot. They were human, but their faces were harsh and cruel, their eyes cold and inhuman. In the next instant they were gone.

"That is a typical scene on the other Earth," the voice of the Cyberene explained.

The scene of the desolate city vanished. In its place appeared another scene. A city under construction. Giant building machines were placing it together, and the parts that were completed were even more beautiful than had been that other city.

Earl, from his vantagepoint, seemed to drop closer and drift over the scene of construction to a part that was inhabited. He saw the people below. They wore no clothes and didn't seem to mind. Each appeared to be intent on going somewhere. None of them were talking or paying any attention to one another. Their expressions were blank, their eyes vacant.

The vantagepoint followed one of them. Shortly the man being followed turned into an archway, up an incline, and into a large hall. He went through a door into the room filled with cell-like vats. In each transparent vat Earl saw a human embryo, alive and growing. He "followed" the man through this place to another, where children were playing with psychological toys designed to increase mechanical and scientific aptitudes.

"This, too, is a typical scene on—this Earth," the Cyberene said. The scene vanished. Once again Earl looked into the video eyes of the Brain. "They are both Earth in the year 3042," the Cyberene said, "but not the *same* Earth. In 1980 there was a split. Earth followed two independent futures. The first, filled with wars and eternal carnage, ever more perfect weapons of destruction, developed from *one* decision you made. The second, my world, filled with perpetual peace and happiness, developed from the alternative decision. *You* created these two futures."

"I?" Earl said. "You must be crazy. How?"

"In the first you discovered the vital nerve fluid that makes me possible. You thought you were God. You thought you could see a future in which I would work the human race harm. You suppressed your discovery by the simple process of giving a negative lab report on the substance. In the second world—*my* world—you did as you were supposed to do. You announced your discovery. *I* came into being."

"You mean to say *my actions* caused the whole planet to split into two identical worlds?"

"In effect, yes. I'll try to explain. Matter and motion are not real in the basic sense. They are properties of your mind. They are what your finite mind sees; but reality is the space-time continuity of which one instant is a cross-section. In effect, consciousness flows along the time dimension, which I term the fourth dimension. But in addition there is a fifth dimension, so that these two Earths have the same space-time coordinates in four dimensions, and two different ones in the fifth. In Euclidean concepts, that other Earth is eighty-seven millionths of an inch from this, in the fifth dimension. In that Earth I did not develop. The Dome is still there, but the Brain, if it still exists, was never activated. As a result, humanity continued its violent progress through time, engaging in war after war.

"When I discovered time travel and saw all this I decided to go back and contact you before your instant of decision and get you to release the identity of the nerve fluid when you discover it *tomorrow*."

"Tomorrow?" Earl said.

"In your time."

"I see," Earl said. "Tomorrow I make the discovery. In one time stream I tell Glassman. In the other I decide not to. *What made me decide not to?*"

"You *thought* the Brain would be bad for humanity. You were, of course, wrong."

"Was I?" Earl said.

"In that other world, wars are the normal state of things. They stem from problems that don't exist in my world. Over-population, competition in trade in things that aren't necessary to human economy, opposed political systems—all the foibles and inconsistencies of untrained and unorganized populations."

"I understand that," Earl said. "Why don't your people wear clothes?"

"Clothes are unnecessary—one of the things I eliminated in reducing the industrial economy to a minimum. Over-population? There is none. People are made in the laboratory as they are needed. Their lives are uncomplicated by animal problems such as reproduction, and artificial customs such as modesty. Their education is simplified and factual, their lives functional."

"And I made that decision all by myself?"

"Yes. That's why I have brought you here—to get you to change that decision. You see, I must change the past. I must do that in order to correct the future, make the other Earth a sane place, *dominated by a second Cyberene which is a counterpart of me.*"

"THAT'S what I thought," Earl said with reckless boldness. "I'm beginning to understand why I made my decision to suppress the identity of the nerve substance. *You* did that. The things I've seen. You're just like dictators of our time. You think you're so right that everyone will naturally agree with you. I don't. I think it's more humane to let people cone into the world as they will and have wars that destroy them, than to decide just how many are to be born. You need a new man in the garbage disposal plant in twenty years? Press a button and he will be born in a few months. Going to have less to do in some factory in twenty years? Keep the zombies from being born. Less trouble than killing them off later to save on the food bill."

"I was afraid you might feel that way," the Cyberene said. "I have the answer to it. Nadine Holmes. Make an accurate report tomorrow on the tests. In return I will leave her in your time—even plant directives so that she will always be a loving and devoted wife to you."

"I would prefer her as she is, naturally."

"Today her every outward manifestation was under my direct mental control. Don't you see, Earl Frye? Just before you followed her into my neatly laid trap to get you here, you watched her come up the hill, and adored every line of her, every mannerism, every play of expression. With one small corner of my mind I can *anticipate* your wishes and fulfill them in her—"

"It wouldn't be *her*," Earl said shaking his head. "And even if it were, at the cost of billions of unborn generations? No."

"But you will do as I wish whether *you* wish to or not. Why not obey me freely and get this reward, rather than nothing?

"*I can control you.*" The voice ended triumphantly.

"No!" It was a shuddering protest from Earl's lips, forcing itself out against his wishes.

The throbbing ache at the base of his brain increased abruptly, slowly, to measurable beats.

"I can control your body, your conscious mind, shoving *you* into the back recesses of thought. And when you try to come out, I can punish you—like I'm doing now."

"No!" Earl screamed, his reserve breaking down completely.

Suddenly, into his cosmos of unbearable suffering and horror, filtered a thought that created hope. Nadine had been *free* during those first hours he had met her. She had defied George Ladd. Unsuccessfully, but she had defied him. And when they had sprawled through that doorway to the future, for a moment he had seen that same *free* Nadine in her eyes, her expression. Or had she ever been free? The terrible throbbing pain blurred his thinking. Had she been free in the smelter where she attracted his attention while the others surrounded him? If he had run directly to her he would have escaped being surrounded. But...

Anger entered his mind like a little finger of thought. Anger at Nadine? He was surprised. Confused. Then it came to him that it was not *his* anger. It came from outside. Alien.

From the depths of his own instincts fear welled up and became blind panic, fighting against the *something* that was growing stronger, crowding around his soul, forcing it to retreat within itself, until Earl Frye, his awareness of being Earl Frye, of being himself, was all that remained, helpless to control or even to feel.

Through a mental fog he was aware that he had stood up, the glass cage had lifted, and he was free to go—but not *he!* His body was controlled by the Cyberene.

He was aware that he had left the dome to walk through a beautifully landscaped garden to a building he had not seen before but which he knew to be the 3042 end of the time tube. He was aware of pausing and looking back at the Dome, now a thing of incredible beauty to him, the repository of his physical vehicle, the Brain. But *not his*. The Cyberene's.

HE entered the time tube. He stepped from it onto grassy ground. He went through the trees to the sidewalk. He returned to the lab building, to his lab, to his living quarters.

He encountered Basil. He listened to himself talk, in casual tones, normal tones. He was unable to control even his conscious thoughts. But his consciousness was a thing apart from him.

He fought the domination of the Cyberene with arms that would not move, with a tongue that would not utter his words, with a rage that would not alter his calm and pleasant expression. He fought the pain that throbbed within him. He fought to stay sane…

Slowly he began to adjust to his position. He no longer fought. He was like a passenger in a plane who watches it take off, fly great distances, and land, with no concern about the details. Having no control whatever over his body, he was free of responsibility toward its routine behavior. He became aware that pain had departed. The very thing he had fought began to interest him. There must be some definite mechanism—property of the mind—that made telepathic enslavement possible in this way. Undoubtedly Nadine was also a free focus of thought behind her enslaved surface.

She came into the lab at ten o'clock, cheerful but impersonal. He heard himself talking to her in the same way. He could see her, listen to her. Therefore, behind her impersonal eyes was the Nadine he had first met, watching him, knowing what had happened. It gave him comfort to know that. He had not lost her. She was *there*.

Knowing that, and knowing there was no way to communicate with her at present, he turned his attention to what her body and his were doing.

"The silicones haven't been explored too thoroughly yet," she was saying. "They have some disadvantages, but those can be eliminated by additions to the ion rings to serve as protective buffers. I have several of them in this tray I brought in. I'd like you to run them through the tests."

Earl's eyes focused on the tray. They paused briefly on the formula of the third one from the nearest end. Earl sensed that this was the long sought for substance. He built up its theoretical structure. He saw at once how it achieved its properties.

"I'll be back this afternoon," Nadine said. "By then you should have your lab reports ready."

Then she was gone. Earl's hands went through the motions of pouring each vial into a pump. He turned his attention away from the routine, as a traveler in a passenger plane might turn from the window to something else.

A feeling of hopelessness grew within him. How could he stop things or interfere with them when he couldn't affect a muscle?

The Cyberene had been playing with him when it tried to get him to do its bidding of his own free will. He realized that now. It would have pleased its vanity if he had.

But this was too important to it for it to trust anything other than itself.

When it was done? When the fluid was forced into the hundreds of thousands of miles of hair-like glass tubing, the billions of fine glass cells? It would never give him his freedom. It would be afraid of what he might be able to do. So it would kill him.

Unless he could prevent the Brain from being activated. And unless he was free to command his body, he could never do that.

What had the Cyberene said to him about time travel and alternate time streams? The theories weren't exactly new. They had been explored in imaginative fiction for over fifty years. No one had really thought there might be some basis in fact for the theories.

What had caused the "split" that had produced two Earths in separate time streams? The Cyberene hadn't seemed to know that detail—or if it had it had brushed over it casually so as not to make him curious about it.

Was it events? Or was it something in the basic substratum of matter, and the events were the result? That might be an important distinction.

If it were events, then bringing the Brain to life in this time stream might eliminate the divergent streams, bringing them together as one. That, in effect, might destroy the other world of 3042 A.D. Maybe that was what the Cyberene intended.

But suppose he was able even yet to defeat the Cyberene's scheme. Then the two time streams would remain unchanged. The free world of the future would remain free. But that was not enough. He wanted to destroy both Brains. How could he accomplish that, assuming he was able to accomplish anything?

THE logical time to do it would be in 1980—now—before the Cyberene gained control of the world and made itself impregnable. But how? And if he could figure that out, could he act if an opportunity arose?

Irene Conner came in at lunchtime. "I had a wonderful time with Basil last night," she sad.

"I'm glad you did," Earl heard his voice say.

Hope leaped within him. Maybe the Cyberene would make some mistake that would arouse suspicions in her. The hope died as the door to the hall opened again and Nadine came in.

"You promised to take me to lunch, Earl," she said.

"Ready," Earl heard himself say.

It was evident that the Cyberene didn't intend him to be alone with any of the others long enough for the possibility of something suspicious to arise.

They went to a small cafe several blocks from the lab building. For the benefit of anyone happening to be looking at them, they carried on small talk while they ate. Earl found himself hanging onto every word Nadine uttered, watching her every expression. He was so close to her, yet so far away. It was like standing outside a window and watching her while she seemed unaware of him.

He kept watching for the faintest flicker of expression that would show the real Nadine. Slowly, without quite realizing it, he began to pretend it was Nadine. He listened to her small talk. He listened to his, and at times forgot it wasn't actually his and that he couldn't control one word of what he said.

He became happy. He let himself be aware of the flavor of the food. He laughed within himself when his vocal cords laughed. He reached out and touched Nadine's hand, thrilling to the feel of her soft skin.

She drew her hand back, a startled light in her eyes. It was gone the next instant. Once more she was impersonal, *controlled*.

The dull, throbbing pain flared to torturing intensity within him, blurring thought, *punishing* him, forcing him behind his prison walls of gray mental fog. But through the pain, apart from it, he experienced a surge of hope. It had been he who had reached out to Nadine. Not the Cyberene controlling him!

Was there still hope? At two o'clock Nadine would pick up his lab report sheets and turn them over to Glassman. Then the identity of the ideal nerve fluid would be known. It would be out of his hands even if he were in full control of his faculties.

He and Nadine rose. They were going back to the lab building. He raged against the hidden mental barriers that contained him. He fought frenziedly to influence some slight movement of his body.

He might as well have been a passenger on an ocean liner trying to change the course of the thousands of tons of steel by thought alone while standing at the rail.

His sphere of awareness grew clouded. He was raging against a mental wall that became almost tangible. He stopped fighting from sheer impotence—and the barrier retreated.

The more I fight the more helpless I am. That thought at once created its corollary. *The less I struggle the closer I am to control.*

That was it! He had so identified his desires with the actions of his body that for one instant he *meshed* with it!

That, then, was the secret. The principle. But it contained within itself its own difficulty. By "wanting" to activate the Brain he could perhaps actually control some of his actions. But the instant he did something counter to the Cyberene, that control would be taken away from him, and replaced by throbbing pain.

He *had* touched Nadine's hand though. It had been a gesture so unconscious that the Cyberene had been unaware of it until it happened.

It was the right direction...

THE possibility of what he wanted to do filled him with a sense of defeat. It would be impossible to falsify the lab report on the nerve fluid. One false word on the card, and the Cyberene would erase it and fill the card out correctly.

He fought back the feeling of futility. He reached out, identifying himself with every sensation from his body. He was walking. He *wanted* to walk. He was talking. He *wanted* to say what he heard himself say.

It would go along well, and then his body would do something he didn't expect, and he would be filled with the realization that he had no control. It would be a mental stumble while his body didn't falter.

During each brief period of identifying his desires with his actions, he found his awareness of sensations expand until it was almost complete identification—complete *meshing*.

Meshing until the gears were almost strong enough to grip—for a brief second. Perhaps in time they would grip for more than a second before alarm bells rang for the Cyberene.

He was alone in his lab. He was placing the fine tubes of test substances in their respective instrument cabinets. Ordinarily he did this almost automatically. Now he watched his every move, building up interest in it, *desiring* to do everything he did, anticipating what he would do next and wanting to do it, pretending it was he who issued the commands to his muscles.

The crucial moment was just ahead. He had stepped to the instrument case that held the key fluid. He started to write down the readings from the instruments. His fingers shook, and it was *his* nervousness that shook them.

A "mistake" in the readings here and there would do it. Speed of ion travel: The meter said two thousand plus feet per second. His fingers wrote the two and a zero. Before he could write the second zero he tried to write the plus sign. Triumphantly he saw his fingers obey his will.

Abruptly they paused—and he was aware that a power outside his will had made them pause.

Throbbing pain surged up to full intensity, enveloping him, sickening him so that his soul was a writhing thing, unable to think or feel anything other than pain. Slowly it lessened—or was he growing better able to suffer it? Thoughts filtered in to him through gray mists clouding his mind.

He saw his hands fill out the rest of the card correctly. He was dimly aware of rushing excitedly from the lab, down the hall, shouting that he had found it.

Others were joining him as he hurried to Glassman's office and burst in, waving the card.

Glassman seized it, his eyes afire with the fulfillment of his Dream.

And it was too late. Too late now to erase the knowledge of the identity of that fluid from Glassman' mind, from the minds of the other nine scientists crowding around him, congratulating him.

It was too late.

That realization crowded out everything else. The Cyberene had won.

CHAPTER SEVEN

"WE want to put it through every test conceivable," Glassman said. "All ten of you drop everything else and work on it. Get the speed of impulse down to the last fraction of an inch per second. Get behavior in different sized tubes. Find the least diameter of the fluid column for nonfunction. Everything. We want to be *sure* before we start pumping two hundred and fifty thousand gallons of the stuff into the Brain."

Dr. Glassman's eyes were afire with the triumph of success. "The dream of my life has come true," he said. "The Brain will live! It will live forever, growing wiser than any man or any group of men. It will remake the world. Civilization. It will end wars. It will guide mankind into a garden of Eden. Utopia. It was my dream for mankind."

He became aware of those watching him. The fire of fanaticism left his eyes. He relaxed, and laughed embarrassedly. "But right now congratulations are in order for Dr. Frye. He's the one who has found the substance that makes it possible."

Nadine had been standing quietly on the sidelines, almost forgotten in this moment. She came forward now and extended her hand. "Congratulations, Dr. Frye," she said.

It was for effect. Earl heard himself say, "Maybe *you* are the one who should get the credit." He paid little attention.

It was a show, an opera, and his body and hers were players reciting lines from a script.

But her hand in his was warm. He clung to the feel of it, thinking bitterly that now there was nothing else. What would become of him? He didn't care.

He sunk into a mood of utter defeat. It was all the worse, he realized, because right now if the Cyberene had not come into the picture, if he had been left to himself, he would be deliriously happy—just as his own exterior self was seeming to be.

After a while he was back in the lab. His body was working on more elaborate experiments with the fluid. His vocal cords were humming a tune in a tone of absent-minded happiness.

He wished fervently that there were some way he could be wiped out completely. Gray walls around his awareness were not enough. Not with the unbearable suffering.

The hours passed slowly for him. He tried not to think, to remain passive. It was no use. His bitterness was too strong. His sense of defeat was too overpowering.

His eyes glanced up at the door as it opened, then down at his wristwatch. It was three minutes after five. Nadine was in the doorway.

"It's time to go Earl," she said.

Go? Where? But his body hastily putting things in order as though it knew.

They left the building together, walked along the sidewalk as though they might be headed toward some dinner rendezvous. They left the sidewalk, and then Earl knew. They were going to the entrance to the time tube. They were going back to the year 3042. Why? He should have remained. Maybe this would create suspicion. But even as he thought that, he knew it wouldn't. Everyone would think he and Nadine were at some restaurant, perhaps later at some nightspot. No one would bother to check and see if he came back to his rooms.

Ahead was the clear spot with its smooth convex depression. And the shimmering refraction in the air. Side by side he and Nadine walked toward it—and were in a corridor, the woodland scene wiped out.

No unusual sensation of any kind. Stepping across a thousand years was no different than crossing the threshold of a doorway.

George Ladd was there waiting for them. "The Cyberene wants to see both of you," he said. Nothing more. No paralysis gun, no guards to keep Earl from escaping. But he couldn't escape. He couldn't move a muscle of his own volition. "Okay," he heard himself say casually.

He and Nadine left the building and went through the beautiful park to the Dome. Inside, they walked along the seemingly roofless slightly curving corridor. He went to a small red square and stood on it. Out of the corner of his eye he saw Nadine do the same. From above, the glass boxes were lowered over them.

Something left him. Without having tested the feeling, he knew that he was in full possession of himself. He could command and his body, his voice, would obey.

He turned toward the glass wall facing Nadine. He pressed against it. She was doing the same.

"Nadine," he said, and it was a greeting, a caress.

"Earl…"

And they were drinking in one another with their eyes.

"VERY touching," a voice said. "One would think you are in love with her, Earl Frye."

"Oh no. I… That is…" Earl stopped in amazement at the self revelation.

"Look at her," the Cyberene's voice said. "In spite of most careful conditioning starting in the lab tank in her pre-breathing stage, she feels the same way about you."

Nadine's lips were trembling with a smile. She was nodding.

Earl was irritated. "Did you bring me here just to tell me that?" he asked. "Or to torture me further?" he added bitterly.

"No. I brought you here to show you that I'm grateful. You did what I wanted done. The fact that it was done in spite of you makes no difference. It's done and can't be undone by you. You realize that?"

"To gloat. I might have known," Earl said contemptuously.

"Not that either. I want to reward you. I've thoroughly explored your mind. I know that if you give your word, you will keep it. I understand a little about your feeling on personal freedom. Now that the vital fluid is known to enough people so that nothing you can do would undo that, I'm willing to let you have Nadine. The real Nadine."

"Yes?" Earl said warily.

"Yes. All I ask in return is your promise not to try to undo anything, and to go ahead with your work without ever mentioning what has happened. Once you give your promise, I will let you and Nadine go to your time and stay there, free agents."

Earl frowned. "I don't get it," he said. "I didn't expect anything like this from you."

"You thought that after I had by-passed you and accomplished my purpose I would eliminate you?" The Cyberene laughed. "You will find that I'm a very benevolent master." The video eyes seemed to glisten with joviality.

"I still don't get it," Earl said, puzzled. "You want my word that I won't interfere with anything you do from here on in."

"Yes. After all, there is a lot to do yet before the Brain in your time stream is activated. I must—"

"So," Earl interrupted. "According to your theory of time that you so carefully explained to me, discovery of the vital nerve substance should have fixed up everything. It didn't."

"The Brain hasn't been activated yet in your time stream. When it has, then the future will reshape itself."

"I want to understand," Earl said. "As I understand it, some act, some *crucial* act, must be changed from the way it happened in the past—in my future in that past. Until that crucial moment is changed from the way it happened, all the future stemming from it remains unaltered. The instant that crucial moment is changed, presto—the whole future from 1980 right down to 3042 does a mighty flip flop and *right here and now*, in that other Earth so close to this one, things will change as abruptly as the change of scene on a screen."

"That's correct."

"Then getting my lab reports correct wasn't the thing. There is still something to come, back there, that must be changed? In spite of everything up to now, you are still facing defeat? That's why you are willing to offer me so much?"

"You misunderstand my motives," the Cyberene said.

"I don't think so. You aren't dealing with a mind-slave now. You may be non-human, but you're a thinking mind. You have desires, motives for doing things, ways of doing them. In other words, you're a type. In offering me everything I want, you're out of your type—unless there's something you want that you can't get any other way. When I came in here I was licked. All I wanted was to die. Now I'm not so sure. I'm not even sure you know what you're doing. I have *hope*. *Do you understand that?"* Earl was trembling violently, a mixture of emotions coursing through him. "I'm going to destroy you before I'm done. You're going to take control of me again and try to prevent that. You don't know whether you can or not because *you can't go into your future.* You can't even go into the past in any detail. How do I know that? I'm a scientist. I'm trained to put two and two together and get four. If you could go anywhere in the past you could have explored every detail of my future and know now what happened."

"Perhaps I do know," the Cyberene said. "You forget I'm attempting to *change* what happened. I have changed what happened. In the time stream the way it was originally, you discovered the right nerve fluid, and suppressed it. You faked a negative report on it. I've changed that much of the past already."

"Have you?" Earl said dully, his emotion spent. "All right then. Don't mind me. You're not going to get any promise from me no matter how much you torture me." His voice changed to cold bitterness. "I'm going to fight you to the end—and win. I don't know how, but the very fact that you haven't changed the present of that other Earth proves you haven't succeeded yet—and won't. *I'll* win. Then I'll destroy you, and Nadine and I can be free."

But somewhere along the line the Cyberene had taken control again. Earl wasn't quite sure when his vocal cords stopped obeying his mental commands.

His body was standing quietly. He could not affect it. The gray walls were closing in around him, the pain growing. He didn't fight it. He welcomed the gray walls that clouded the channels to his conscious mind.

He sensed dimly that he and Nadine were going back the way they had come. Back to the time tube. Back to 1980, to what might be the final battle.

He was alone in his living quarters. He was aware of sleeping. Then it was morning, and he crept cautiously into his conscious mind, a hurt and wounded soul. And his conscious mind was serene and happy, unaware of his suffering as it began its day's work.

"HI, Earl."

Earl looked up with a smile. "Hello, Basil. How's things going with you and Irene?"

Basil smiled wryly. "Well…at least she's discovered that I'm a pretty fair dancer. She envies you. I guess I do too. You have all the luck."

"Nonsense! Discovering the right substance was like winning the Irish Sweepstakes."

"That's what I mean. You did nothing more than any of the rest of us. It was pure chance that the right stuff was in a tray given to you to test. But in the history books your name will get the credit—just like it took brains."

Earl shrugged. "I'm afraid all our names will be left out. Dr. Glassman will get the credit. He masterminded the whole thing. He deserves the credit, too. The rest of us are just damned good chemists. That's all. He took the risks. If it it hadn't paid off, the Dome would have been known as Glassman's Folly."

"Something in that," Basil said. "By the way, what have you found out about Nadine? You two seem quite palsy walsy now."

"She's what she claims to be," Earl said.

"Is she?" Basil said, his eyes narrowing. "I think you're lying. Matter of fact, you're different than you were. What's come over you?"

"Nothing, Basil."

"Nothing, he says," Basil said mournfully to the bench he was sitting on. "What happened to you? Have you been bought?"

"What do you mean?"

"You know what I mean. Nadine came here under mysterious circumstances, to say the least. You were hot on the trail of something. You wanted me to help you follow her. I couldn't, because Irene had given me my first chance to date her. So you followed her by yourself. What happened?"

"Sure," Earl said. "She went to the best hotel in town. I called her on a house phone and asked her to have dinner with me. She did."

"Did she tell you how she happened to be only four inches high and naked when you first met her?"

Earl stared at Basil in mock astonishment. "Basil," he said softly. "Haven't you ever heard of that terrible scourge of the human race—alcohol?"

"Don't give me that!" Basil said, his nostrils flaring. "You were stone sober. I was with you for an hour while you bought those clothes and patiently gathered fashion magazines that would show a dame who didn't know the first thing about it how to put them on. I saw Nadine in this lab, being carried off by a man. I was paralyzed by a ray gun or something from a gun. So were you."

"He's right, Earl."

Both men turned toward the door. It was Nadine. She closed the door and came into the lab.

"Maybe we should take him with us, Earl," she said. "If we don't, he's going to think the worst things about us. I know we swore you to secrecy, but he could wreck everything."

"Maybe you're right," Earl said.

"Oh no," Basil said, edging toward the door. "They *did* something to you, Earl.. I'm not going to give them a chance to do the same thing to me."

"Don't be a fool," Earl said. "Let me at least explain things."

NADINE was edging toward the door to cut off Basil's escape. He saw this, and leaped past her to the door, pulling it open.

"Come back here and let me explain," Earl heard himself say.

"You can explain to the Secret Service," Basil said.

He shut the door on them. An impulse made him turn toward Dr. Glassman's office. He would tell him first, and if that didn't get results he would go to the S. S. boys.

He knocked on Glassman's door and pushed it open without waiting for an invitation.

"Dr. Glassman," he said quickly, "something very suspicious is going on around here. I should have told you about it sooner, but I thought Earl would be able to explain his actions, and Nadine's. Have you looked into her credentials? She isn't what she claims. I know, but I don't know how I'm going to prove it right now. She's done something to Earl. He isn't the same. They're in this together."

"Just a minute, Dr. Nelson," Glassman cut in. "Are you trying to say that Dr. Frye and Dr. Holmes are in on some mad scheme to sabotage the Brain? You must be mad. Why, Dr. Frye discovered the chemical we've spent close to a million dollars searching for!"

"I know that," Basil said doggedly, "but just the same—"

"You're out of your mind. What are you trying to do? Curry favor with me at the expense of innocent and hard working people? I've a good notion to discharge you on the spot."

"You've got to listen to—"

"Get out. I'll hear no more of it."

Basil stared at him blankly, then nodded. "All right," he said, "but you're going to have to listen later. I'm taking it to the Secret Service. They'll have to listen."

He backed out, closing the door on Glassman's angry face. When he turned to go down the hall he saw Earl and Nadine coming toward him. With them was George Ladd, his right hand in his suit coat pocket over something bulging—the paralysis gun, maybe.

Basil turned the other way and down another hall, running with a speed born of fear and determination. He knew now he had been right.

A door opened. Irene came out, almost bumping into him. "Where are you going in such a hurry, Basil?" she demanded.

"Can't explain now," he said. She stood in his way. "Come with me," he said desperately. "I'll explain on the way. Hurry."

She nodded. Together they ran down the hall and reached the side exit. Taking Irene's hand, Basil plunged away from the sidewalk through scattered trees, until they reached the parking lot. He unlocked his car with shaking fingers and told Irene to get in. He rushed around to the driver's side.

The motor caught instantly. He started with a clash of gears. In the rear view mirror he saw George Ladd running toward him. Then he reached the street—and almost immediately was slowed by heavy traffic.

Groaning under his breath, he made the best time he could. Irene watched him silently for two blocks.

"Aren't you going to tell me what it is?" she asked abruptly.

"He's after me," Basil said. "We've got to get there before he can stop me. You can listen when I tell the Secret Service about it."

Ahead was a traffic jam. Basil turned into a side street where he made better time. It was taking him forever to get there. But finally his destination was just ahead. The office building where the S. S. had its local office.

There was a parking space. Basil swerved toward it and braked to a stop. He reached past Irene and opened her door.

"Get out and run for it," he said.

The screech of tires almost drowned his voice. He looked over his shoulder. A car had pulled up beside his in the street. He saw George Ladd behind the wheel, alone.

Frantically, Basil pushed Irene out and followed her, taking her hand as they ran toward the building entrance fifteen feet away.

"We've got to make it," he said. "We've got to…"

There was no sound, no light, from the weapon George Ladd pointed at them.

Basil sprawled forward. Before he hit the sidewalk, flame burst from his hair, his clothing.

Irene stopped, forgetting her danger or not knowing it. She bent down by Basil, reaching to help him. She remained in that position for a long second while her hair and clothing burst into flames, then crumpled against him.

Horrified pedestrians drew back from the bodies, the stench of seared flesh. In the street a motor roared into life. The car with George Ladd sped away.

EARL turned away from the window. "George Ladd just brought my car back," he said. "I guess he isn't coming in. He's walking into the woods toward the tube entrance."

Nadine nodded casually.

Within his mental prison Earl worried. What had Ladd done? He wouldn't dare to kill Basil. The worst that could happen would be that Basil would be taken before the Cyberene and made into a mind-slave too.

There were footsteps in the hall. The door opened. It was Dr. Glassman, his lips set in a grim line.

"Dr. Frye," Glassman said. "Basil came to me with a story of something going on he didn't like. He accused you and Dr. Holmes of some scheme to sabotage the Brain."

"That's utter nonsense," Earl heard himself say.

"Why, I can't understand—" Nadine began.

"I thought so too," Glassman said, "until I received a telephone call from the police just now. Basil and Irene were killed a few moments ago while on their way to try to get the Secret Service to listen to what I refused to hear."

"Oh," Nadine said without expression. Earl said nothing. He was too stunned to think.

"I'm going to get to the bottom of this," Glassman went on grimly. "You may both consider yourselves relieved of your duties until the Secret Service has investigated thoroughly. Save your explanations until I've called them."

Earl tried to warn Glassman. He forced his lips open to call to him—and a wave of searing throbbing pain lashed at him, forcing him back behind the gray fog.

Through the mental haze he saw George Ladd in the doorway, a thirty-eight Colt automatic in his hand—something Glassman would understand.

"Come with me, Dr. Glassman," Ladd said expressionlessly.

WHEN Glassman returned an hour later, to all outward appearances he was unchanged, except that he made no mention of the deaths of Basil and Irene. Nor did he say anything about suspending Earl and Nadine.

From his own experience Earl knew that one part of Glassman was raging against his mental prison, perhaps feeling the sadistic torture with which the Cyberene kept him chained.

By a supreme effort Earl pulled himself away from thinking about what had happened. It multiplied his determination to free himself enough to defeat the Cyberene and destroy it. But raging impotently against the Brain's control wouldn't accomplish a thing.

Little by little he willed himself back to a frame of thought where he could reach out into his conscious mind again, matching his thoughts and moods with it. It had somehow "forgotten" much of what had happened to Basil and Irene and Glassman. It was thinking about Nadine.

Earl thought about her too. She loved him. She didn't know what love was, but it was there, revealed in the brief moment she had been free to express herself. Was that love now making her try to overthrow the slavery of the Cyberene? Probably not. She was conditioned to accept that inhuman intellect as her master.

Earl shoved the real Nadine from his thoughts and dwelt on the Nadine that was manifest. She was easy to love, too— and why not? She was everything that the true Nadine was— except that she was not the *complete* Nadine. She was falling in love with him, too. And his own conscious mind was in love with her. Why not make the most of it?

He inserted the idea into his conscious thoughts, and to his delight no alarm bells rang. The Cyberene didn't interfere.

"Let's go to a dance tonight after work," he said.

"A dance? I don't know how to dance."

"I'll teach you. It isn't hard to pick up."

"All right," Nadine said.

Earl worked hard the rest of the day. Tank trucks were bringing the nerve fluid to the Dome in a never-ending stream. Every load had to be tested before it was unloaded into the storage tanks, to make sure its quality was up to standard. One five thousand-gallon load could contaminate it all.

At six o'clock he was relieved of his work. He dressed eagerly, finding no difficulty in *meshing* one hundred percent with the desires of his conscious mind. He picked up Nadine at her hotel.

Crestmont boasted only two places worth going. One was just a dance floor, the other The Barn, with a small orchestra and dinners.

"The orchestra isn't as good here at The Barn," Earl said when they went in, "but we can have a table and enjoy ourselves."

They ordered their dinner. The orchestra started playing and soon the floor was fairly crowded. Earl took Nadine's hand and led her to the dance floor. After a few steps she discovered that she could dance quite easily. It delighted her.

They returned to their table finally, and ate. Afterward they danced again. Two of the other scientists were there with their partners. They nodded at Earl and Nadine but didn't join them.

During all this, Earl was careful not to insert any feeling, any impulse of his own into his conscious mind. What he intended to do must come as a surprise to both Nadine and the Cyberene, and afterwards they must think it to be the product of that conscious mind—not Earl himself.

His opportunity arose naturally. While they were dancing he spoke to her. She lifted her face to smile at him. Swiftly he kissed her, letting his lips linger until the throbbing and an angriness beat into him and a power outside himself pulled him back.

He retreated in his mind, afraid even to think, lest the Cyberene sense his thoughts and realize what he had been trying.

"Why did you do that?" he heard Nadine say from a great distance, through waves of torture.

His own voice replied, "That was a kiss."

"How...disgusting," Nadine said.

Had she meant that? Or were those just words put in her mouth by the Cyberene.

"It's one of our customs," Earl's voice said. "Watch the others on the dance floor. Quiet! See that couple over at the corner table?"

Earl crept cautiously into his conscious mind to watch Nadine. She studied the couple, puzzled. She looked up into his face thoughtfully and began dancing again. "Maybe," she said, "it won't seem so disgusting if we try it again."

Her lips parted. Earl felt his head bend toward her. He felt the kiss, but held himself cautiously alert for the first sign of disapproval from the Cyberene. It didn't come.

The moment passed. Earl began to relax. Had the Cyberene assumed it was a natural action of his conscious mind divorced from him? If so, then a major hurdle had been met successfully.

"It is rather pleasant," Nadine said. Then, thoughtfully, "So that's a kiss."

Earl looked at her sharply. Was it possible that the real Nadine had caused those words to be spoken? Maybe. It provided a new avenue of speculation. Had Nadine long ago discovered what he was so patiently trying now—how to circumvent the control of the Cyberene? She could have, but not seeing any reason to do so, kept her talent hidden...

CHAPTER EIGHT

TWO more days passed. Earl forgot his caution and boldly cooperated with his conscious mind on the many tasks that took up his time. And strangely he was almost free of pain, though it never entirely left.

Dr. Glassman took all the scientists with him on a tour of inspection within the Brain. The millions of fine glass tubes and hollow bulbs that comprised the Brain would soon start being filled with nerve fluid. Although tons of pressure per square inch were required to force it into the tubes, once there, capillary attraction pulled it along.

On the first trip Earl retreated from his conscious mind as much as possible, while still watching everything around him closely. He had been inside the Brain many times before—but never with any thought of discovering a weakness where it could be destroyed.

That was the task he had set himself. It was an almost impossible one. Destroying the Brain now, in 1980, might not accomplish his purpose. The damage could be repaired.

He thought of dynamite and rejected it. It would deteriorate long before 3042, and even if it remained potent, it would do no more than damage a small part of the Brain—not enough to more than partially impair its thinking or give it a case of specialized forgetfulness. A dynamite explosion in such an enormous brain would be equivalent to a blood clot on a human brain.

Nothing better presented itself to him on that first trip. Was he going to fail?

The next day pumping of the nerve fluid began. The masses of hair-fine glass tubing lost their appearance of glass wool and began to appear as individual threads of yellowish orange.

It would be many days before the "loading", as it was termed, would be completed, but everyone was kept busy watching it, and catching broken threads as they started to ooze fluid, sealing them with a special formula sealer.

During these days a dozen plans to destroy the Brain occurred to Earl. Each had its defects that would make it fail. As the "loading" neared its last day, only one possibility remained.

Great precautions had been taken to make the Brain free from vibration. The slightest sound of almost any frequency, if continued long enough, would find a nerve strand that would vibrate to it and snap.

A loudspeaker broadcasting at full power over the entire range of sound would be more devastating to the Brain than a ton of dynamite exploded in its heart. There was the answer—Vibration!

But once again there was the problem of installing it, and being able to use it after a thousand years. Install it and use a clock to trigger it? That was one possibility. Clocks run by atomic power would keep accurate time over much longer periods.

But there was the problem of getting the Cyberene to agree to the installation of such a device. That was necessary. During the days that Earl had studied the Cyberene's control of his conscious mind he had found no way to gain any sort of positive control, which the Cyberene couldn't shunt out at once. Therefore whatever plan he devised must meet with the approval of the Cyberene.

Tentatively he inserted a bold thought, feeling sure that the Cyberene wouldn't attribute it to him, but merely to the logical processes of his conscious mind.

What if the Brain doesn't develop along lines sympathetic to you? He elaborated upon it, feeding worry thoughts along with it. A second Brain might not follow the line of development of the first, any more than one human develops like another, even when they are twins. Rather than accomplishing his aim of having a second Cyberene on the other Earth in 3042, holding the human population in slavery, it might prove a more formidable enemy than the people of that Earth. And if that turned out to be the case, wouldn't it be better to have a trump card? Some way of destroying the second Cyberene at any time? Even if it were friendly to the first, it might want to be boss. Power of life and death over it would prevent that.

Earl's conscious mind, entirely cooperative with the Cyberene, soon began to think very dominantly along those lines. Earl sat back and waited for some reaction from the Cyberene. It was not long in coming.

At five o'clock Nadine looked him up and informed him that they were to report to the Cyberene at once.

"I HAVE detected certain thoughts in your mind," the voice of the Cyberene sounded. "I would like to hear what you have to say."

Earl sensed his mind rallying its thoughts, "I've been wondering what the other Cyberene would be like. That's all. There's no guarantee that it will have any special traits that will make it what you want it to be, and once it's started it's out of your control, isn't it?"

"That's true. Time travel and even fifth dimension travel is extremely limited. Once the other Cyberene is generated, I can't contact it until 3042—now."

"Can you look into your future and see—"

"Unfortunately, no. I can't even see into your tomorrow. I might, perhaps, jump to the year 4104 A. D., but even that is beyond my present ability and instruments. It may be many centuries before I understand everything about hyperspace."

"That's what I surmised," Earl heard himself say. He stole a glance at Nadine, who was watching him attentively. "That's why I think, for your own protection, you should be able to destroy the other Cyberene instantly—if it isn't what you hope it will be."

"How?" The Cyberene's voice was vibrant with eagerness.

"The basic device would be sound vibrations in the air, inside its braincase. A loud continuous sound of nearly all frequencies would cause billions of nerve strands to vibrate, and enough of them would break to destroy the functioning of the whole. That could be built into it in 1980. The problem is to decide how to trigger it. Do you have any ideas?"

"It's very simple," the Cyberene said. "It will never forget once it learns something. Before its mind integrates into a self-aware ego, attach a relay to some motor outlets. Decide on some key combination of sounds that might be spoken. Repeat them into the auditory centers of the Brain, at the same time tripping the relay. Keep doing that until utterance of the sequence of sounds causes the relay to trip. When that response is automatic, connect the relay to the loudspeaker. Once you have done that, report to me. Then all I need do is contact the second Cyberene, in this age, and if I want to destroy it I can repeat the sounds."

Earl, in his mental cubicle, chuckled. He could not have thought of a better way himself.

"And," the Cyberene said, "in order to account for your task, you had better 'sell' Glassman on the idea. Tell him it's so that *mankind* can destroy the Brain if necessary. But make sure no one in 1980 knows the key sounds. You may return to 1980."

"I'VE had much the same thought," Victor Glassman said, chewing on his lip. "I rather hated to think about it

72

though. Destroy my Creation? Still, I suppose it's wise—to be *able* to." He stood up and came around from behind his desk.

Earl and Nadine watched without speaking as he clasped his hands behind his back and went to the window of his office, which brought him a view of part of the giant dome, housing the Brain.

"Every precaution is being taken otherwise. Until we can be sure of ourselves we don't intend letting the Brain have control of any machines or weapons. Of course we could forget that danger, in time, and suddenly wake up to the fact that we were too late. Then it would be nice to still be able to... All right. Go ahead. Keep it under your hats though. And when you're done we can form a select group, handing the—" he smiled wryly—"password down from generation to generation."

"I have the plans all drawn up," Earl said. "An electrostatic speaker, because it can be built with parts that will last forever. No moving parts in the frequency generator or amplifier. Leads to the permanent busses that will supply current for such things as video eyes and the voice speaker system..."

"Good. Good. Only we will indoctrinate that Mind early so that it will never do anything detrimental to us."

"Of course," Earl soothed. "This is only precautionary."

DAYS followed one another swiftly. A factory-made electrostatic loudspeaker arrived, and was dismantled so that some of its parts could be replaced with more durable ones. Specifications for the frequency generators and the amplifier were farmed out, and the completed units arrived.

There was trouble with the relay. It was well designed, but there was doubt whether it would still be in working condition after ten centuries. Earl sent specifications to a jewelry manufacturer in Kansas City and had its moving parts made of synthetic ruby and platinum.

The Cyberene *watched* every step of construction—and so did Earl, from within his artificially created mental wall, careful not to reveal the huge holes he had knocked in it.

With the arrival of the remade relay, Earl and Nadine entered the Brain, setting up a vibration-proof chassis in its innermost heart where the maze of fine spun glass was now a maze of yellowish threads containing a fluid with exactly the same properties as human nerve fluid.

Outside, swarming over the catwalks and dotting the immense corridor circling the Brain, were dozens of technicians and experts, beginning the task of barraging the gigantic man-made brain with a never ending sequence of visual and audible sensory impressions, which according to theory, would eventually synthesize that miracle of creation loosely known as thought in the thousands of tons of glass and nerve fluid.

Using a portable low power microscope and the techniques he had acquired during the months of work on the Brain in its construction, Earl attached motor buds to randomly chosen nerves, and sensory buds to others, attaching them to the transistors that would feed the relay, so that the action of the relay would set up nerve impulses n the Brain. When it had been done, he used sensitive detectors to make sure ion currents were generated in the nerves.

Where those nerve impulses went to among the billions of "brain cells" didn't matter. All that mattered was that they went *somewhere*, so that the basic property of association would "hook them on" to the auditory impression created by speaking the code word or sequence of code sounds.

"What should we use as the code sounds?" Nadine asked as their task neared completion.

"I've been trying to think of something," Earl said.

And in his mental prison Earl had been trying to think of the same thing, keeping track of his conscious mind's thoughts on the subject—even influencing them at times.

It would have to be a sequence of sounds that stood no chance whatever of being spoken to the Brain during the next thousand years. Otherwise they might be spoken by chance and the Brain destroyed.

"How about nonsense syllables?" Nadine suggested.

Earl grinned. "Those are the most dangerous of all. Take Y.M.C.A. It's the initials of a huge organization. Any nonsense sequence of letters, no matter how long, might someday be the letters of some organization."

Nadine frowned in bewilderment. "But what else is there? If we take any sequence of sensible words, they might be repeated in reference to something else at any time."

"Not if they're *very* special," Earl said, and it was the real Earl Frye, almost completely out of his mental walls and daring discovery recklessly, who was speaking now.

An impish light glowed in Nadine's eyes, making Earl almost sure that the real Nadine had sensed long ago what he was doing and had done the same, *meshing* cautiously with her conscious mind until at times, camouflaged by its normal thoughts, she could *appear*.

"Kiss me, Earl Frye," she said, lifting her face toward his.

"The pleasure is all mine, Nadine Holmes," he said, cupping her face in his hands and pressing his lips to hers. "And that's what I mean," he murmured through imprisoned lips. "No one else, through all the ages, will say those words, let alone say them in the same way."

She drew back. "No!" she said abruptly. "The Cyberene has promised that we can stay in your time, free to do as we please. That would mean that we would have to be in the future—in *my* time."

"But only until the Cyberene could make sure," Earl said, glad that she had made that objection. It would allay the Cyberene's suspicions if it had any.

A telepathed thought impinged on Earl's mind, and from Nadine's expression, on hers too. *Earl is right, I have thought of the problem of what the key sound should be. He has hit on the right answer. It must be your voices, filled with emotion, speaking those words you just spoke.*

Again Earl relaxed with a mental sigh of relief. He had reached his goal. There was nothing more for him to do now, except wait. His conscious mind would carry on the details under the supervision of the Cyberene.

A MICROPHONE was brought into the Brain, already attached to the auditory centers of the Brain. Earl examined the microphone, then went in search of another type. "We must have one with a contact button on it," he explained, "so that just the key words impinge on the Brain when we close the relay manually."

At last everything was ready. "Now," Earl said.

Nadine lifted her face and closed her eyes. "Kiss me, Earl Frye;" she said.

Earl released the button. "That isn't the way," he said. "Imagine we are alone in the universe, and we are about to die. Imagine swirling mists about to envelope you and drag you away from me forever, and this is the last kiss you'll ever get…"

"Oh, no," Nadine whispered, opening her eyes wide. "That must never happen. The Cyberene has promised!"

"Close your eyes and imagine it is," Earl said. "Close your eyes. Now—there are swirling mists. Your world of dreams has crashed around you. Ahead is—destruction. You can't escape it. It's coming, closer. You're going to die, but before you do you want—"

"Kiss me, Earl Frye," Nadine said.

"That's it. Say it again." Earl pressed the mike button.

"Kiss me, Earl Frye…"

Earl closed his eyes. It was the end. In another moment he would die. He had failed. He held this in his mind's eye. With a mixture of sadness and tenderness, and bitterness, he said, "The pleasure is all mine, Nadine Holmes," and tripped the relay with his fingers.

Would it work? After the hundredth try he began to wonder. But the repeated words with their inflections, their subtle differences in repetition, had to build up in the Brain, synthesize, associate with the sensation of the tripping of the relay—and *connect*. There was as yet no *mind* functioning in that mass of glass and nerve fluid. No ready made paths to coordinated concepts, conscious thought.

It was the next day before his fingers felt the relay trip of its own accord. *Drama*, he thought, feeling the thrill of that sentient movement. He said nothing to Nadine, not wanting to end their game. And the next time the relay didn't trip. And the next. But the next time it did, and the next and the next…

CHAPTER NINE

"YOU'RE done?" Dr. Glassman said, rubbing his hands in great satisfaction. He lowered his voice to a whisper. "What is the code word?"

Earl winked at Nadine, then looked around in a pretense at making sure no one could hear. "We picked L.S.M.F.T.," he whispered. "I figured that since a cigarette company had used that in its advertising years ago, it would never be used again by anybody."

"Excellent!" Glassman beamed. "Excellent! To think that by uttering those five letters this entire project, representing millions of dollars—before it's a completely integrated Mind—can be *shattered*." He looked around him, exuding a sense of his newly acquired power.

"And," Earl said ruefully, "I guess that winds up everything for me in Project Brain, doesn't it? I hope so. I could use a vacation."

Dr. Glassman looked slyly from Earl to Nadine. "Are congratulations in order?"

Earl bent swiftly and whispered in Glassman's ear, "I haven't asked her yet. I wanted to wait until our work was over. You know, business before pleasure."

"Ha ha," Glassman chuckled knowingly, looking at Nadine with an I-know-a-secret look. "You're a man after my own heart, Earl." Then, more soberly, "Yes, I guess you are due for a vacation. And your consultant duties are finished, Dr. Holmes. I'll miss both of you."

Earl and Nadine left Glassman outside the Brain, and returned to the lab annex. They didn't speak as they walked down the hall to Earl's lab. They stood just inside the door, looking over the scene of machines and instruments and tables and bottles, which had been their surroundings for so long.

Earl looked at the lab table where he had first seen Nadine, so many days—it seemed ages—ago. He would never see this place again. He entertained no illusions about the future. The Cyberene would never permit them to return to 1980.

With heavy feet he went across the lab to his living quarters. He began packing, and Nadine sat on the arm of a chair, watching.

"What are you doing?" she asked.

"Packing my belongings to take with us," Earl said.

"Oh, but you don't need to do that. We'll be back in a few hours—a day or two at the most. The Cyberene has promised. Just as soon as it makes sure it doesn't need us."

"Sure," Earl said, "but I'll take them just the same. Then when we come back we can go straight to the airport and catch a plane to Miami or someplace and get married."

Fifteen minutes later they left the lab. They walked along the familiar sidewalk to the spot where they always cut through the woods toward the hill, circling it so no one would know where they had gone.

They reached the clearing. Ahead, shimmering in the evening sun, was the familiar refractive outline in the atmosphere. There was no breeze to stir the still leaves. A meadowlark broke the silence with its call, and was silent. Over the trees the giant dome that housed the Brain loomed, unbelievable in its enormous bulk.

Nadine took his hand and stopped him. "Kiss me, Earl Frye," she said, her lips trembling.

Earl looked down at her upturned face. Did she know? Perhaps the real Nadine, within, sensed what was to come.

Or perhaps she didn't.

The tom tom beat of pain began within him. He forced his way through it, taking her into his arms.

"The pleasure is all mine, Nadine Holmes," he murmured.

Their lips met, tenderly, then crushed together with the fierceness of passion.

Their lips parted, lingeringly, regretfully. They drew back, to look into each other's eyes for a brief moment, a moment Earl knew the Cyberene had given them to make more bitter what was to come.

Earl saw the glow fade from Nadine's eyes. As he picked up his suitcases he heard someone appoaching.

Victor Glassman joined them, his face gray, his expression wooden.

This was it. Glassman might be missed. There might be an investigation, but Project Brain would go on regardless of that now. And the only ones who might stop it were here.

Side by side they walked toward the barely perceptible refractive shimmer. Beyond it they could see the woodland, a Bluejay's flashing wings, a chipmunk standing upright, observing them. And then they were standing in the familiar hall, in the year 3042.

George Ladd was not there, but there was no need for him to be there. Their bodies, controlled by the Mind that enslaved them, walked on toward the far exit and the garden they would cross—to the Dome, the Cyberene.

THERE was no turning back now. Nor would there be other days to perfect the technique of *meshing* with his mind. Earl reached out into every part of his thoughts, thinking them, identifying himself with them, with the desires of the Cyberene. In that other Earth so close to this there would now be a Second Cyberene. There must be, since nothing stood in the way of its developing throughout the ten centuries and more since they had left it, a few minutes ago.

They entered the garden and paused. Earl dropped his two suitcases beside the path. He took Nadine's hand in his. They went on toward the portal that led into the Dome.

They walked down the silent circling corridor under the network of catwalks and ladders, past panels of instruments whose needles fluctuated with life, to the red squares over, which hung the glass cages, ready to be lowered. Would they be lowered, separating them from each other while they faced the Cyberene?

The glittering lenses of the two video cameras moved as they went toward them, keeping them in line.

"All of you occupy one square," the Cyberene's voice instructed.

They obeyed without sign of emotion. The glass cage was lowered over them. Its front wall became a window through which they were looking at the familiar Dome.

But it was a structure around which weeds grew in thick profusion, with its acres of exposed surface pitted by time, untended.

"What happened?" Earl said. "Do you mean to say that there is still something to be done?"

"There is nothing to be done," the Cyberene said dully. "I have checked in that other time stream. There is still positive record that the Brain was not activated."

"Maybe it takes time for the momentum of events to force the change," Earl suggested.

Didn't the Cyberene suspect yet? Didn't it *realize?*

"No," the Cyberene said dully. "I have failed. More, I have rechecked the mathematical basis of the theoretical picture, and think I know where I erred. The cause of the split that created two Earths, travelling close together down through so many centuries, could not have been something occurring in the original time stream. It took something applied from the fifth dimension—and in the neighborhood of the split that could only have been one thing, *the force with which the time tube hooked onto 1980.* It had to be that. The accident. I didn't take it into account."

"That's what I've thought all along," Earl said quietly.

"At that instant," the Cyberene went on as though it hadn't heard him, "the split occurred. You became two Earl Fryes, to mention one facet of the split. One of you went its way, making an accurate report of its experiments, creating me eventually—"

While the Cyberene talked, the desolate scene vanished, and the glass cage lifted upward slowly, as though it were a curtain, lifting for the final scene.

The twin lenses of the Cyberene's video eyes were fixed on them, alive with an intelligence that was unhuman.

"No," Earl said. *"That* one of me discovered the identity of the nerve substance, but suppressed it."

"That couldn't be," the Cyberene objected. "Nothing appeared in its life to cause it to do that. You were the one who had the data to make such a decision."

"But I reported accurately," Earl said. *Even yet it didn't see!*

"I know," the Cyberene said, "but it can't be, because then that electrostatic speaker would be—" It stopped.

"Deep inside of you," Earl continued. "Waiting only for—"

A WAVE of emotion blasted into his mind, driving him by its very force into the deep recesses behind his wall of gray, into a cosmos of mind wrenching pain.

"No!" the thought blasted into him. "No human can have the power to destroy me! It can't exist. *You* can't exist another instant, with the danger to me!"

In agony Earl reached out, meshing little by little with his conscious mind, *feeling* its terror and fear of death, calming it, controlling it with all the infinite skill he had learned during the past weeks.

And even as he gained control against the will of the Cyberene he realized with a sinking feeling the essential weakness of his plan. Nadine!

He had been criminally stupid, blinded by emotion toward her. She was conditioned from birth to accept the domination of the mind of the Cyberene.

Sweating with the terrible effort it took to hold on, he forced his muscles to permit him to turn toward her. His worst fears were realized. She stood there, her face a calm mask that revealed no emotion.

Abruptly the raging force of thought and searing torture from the Cyberene calmed. In its place was cold triumph.

"So you have been able to defeat me in your own mind," it said. "You made *your* error in calculation, too. Nadine Holmes. She is mine."

"Nadine Holmes?" It was Nadine who uttered the two words, her lips trembling with terrible effort, beads of sweat dotting her smooth forehead.

Hope surged into Earl's thoughts. "But you can't allow her to live either, can you?" he said. "In another moment you must destroy us both, so that nothing can ever threaten your existence. We will have only another minute or two before you reach into us, plunging us into the gray swirling fists of death, where we will be separated forever. *There is no way we can avoid that now, is there?*"

Nadine had turned toward Earl, every muscle of her slim body protesting under the domination of the Cyberene. Earl was forgotten by the Brain as it concentrated on the battle against Nadine.

She held out her arms, perspiring with the effort. "Kiss me, Earl Frye," she whispered.

A blast of fear flowed into Earl's mind. He fought to the surface of thought, clinging there, calming himself. But defeat was close—impossible to avoid.

It had been a wonderful plan to destroy this thing that ruled the minds of men, making them its slaves. Resistance was useless. In another moment he would be dead.

Bitterly, hopelessly, with infinite sadness, he said, as though somewhere long ago he had repeated it before, a tender ritual whose meaning now escaped him, "The pleasure is all mine, Nadine Holmes…"

Their lips met with the tenderness of farewell.

A *SOUND* came into being, seeming to come from far away, yet seeming to exist everywhere, with no point of origin. It was at the same time a deep rumble and an insane, high screaming—and every sound in between that had ever been uttered by voice or machine or unleashed elements in desolate places. It was soulless, yet holding within itself the torment of every lost soul since the beginning of time.

It forced its way into Earl's consciousness, hung there as though stopped by some hidden barrier. Abruptly it swept forward, and as it swept into the farthest reaches of Earl's mind it washed away throbbing pain, the sense of inescapable doom, leaving *a sense of freedom*—a clean freshness, an emotion of peace.

A rapid coruscation of words, syllables, and sounds whispered and blasted from the voice box of the Cyberene as neural circuits within the Brain snapped or short-circuited.

Earl and Nadine lifted their heads in startled surprise and a new awakening. They saw the glittering lens eyes that had been watching them jerk spasmodically. Within the lens of one electronic eye a flash of blue fire exploded. Then both eyes became motionless, dead, pointed in different directions.

Overhead, giant blinding bolts of unleashed current leaped from copper bars to catwalks. The smell of molten and burning metal filled the air. Then, as though cut off by some hidden hand, the unholy sound within the Brain stopped. The arcing surges of electric power in the catwalks and power lines overhead stilled.

There was silence, and motionless clouds of white and gray smoke.

It took a moment for Earl to realize that in defeat he had won. It took another moment for him to realize that it was not he who had won, but Nadine—her love for him—a love that had grown in a girl who had never known that love existed.

There was no doubt of it now as he watched the play of expression that crossed her face. Fear, doubt, hope, desperate hope, living hope, love, fear, then all the love that had developed within her, shining from her face with the spiritual brilliance of a brilliant sun.

"Earl!" It was a glad cry. She clung to him as though she would never let him go.

For that matter, she would never need to, he thought, as he drew her closer. They would need each other for the rest of their lives. Or for a dozen lifetimes if they could have that many.

"My God!" The words exploded into their minds. They had been uttered by Dr. Glassman, and they contained all the horror, the comprehension of everything that had happened that the mind-enslavement had given to him.

"It's over now," Earl said. "The Cyberene is dead."

Glassman shook his head vigorously. "It should never have existed in the first place," he said. "All my dreams of what it could do to help humanity... We've got to destroy the Brain in 1980, before any of this can happen."

Earl shook his head, looking at Nadine. "Nadine and I are staying here," he said quietly. "There's work to do that only we can do. People, their minds freed for the first time, bewildered, needing to be led a little ways into the path of freedom until they can care for themselves. A future to build—from 3042."

"You can stay if you must," Glassman said, his voice vibrant with the shock and horror of what he had experienced, "but I'm going back—to prevent this 3042 from ever happening. I can do it. I can trip that relay manually. It will destroy—" His voice broke. "—my life's work. But it has to be done."

He turned and ran blindly.

EARL made no move to stop him. He watched him vanish around the bend of the corridor, waiting fatalistically. Would the scientist be able to wipe out this time-stream? Deep within him, Earl felt it couldn't be done. The Cyberene had tried to change the past, and failed.

Perhaps the Cyberene had been wrong in what it believed had caused the split in time that produced two Earths. Maybe one part of Glassman would be unable to bring itself to destroy its Creation, the Brain. Maybe that's what had happened. Maybe Glassman, torn between two opposed decisions, had been able to act on neither...

Earl put his arm around Nadine. They walked slowly along the curving corridor, circling the dead Brain, going toward the outside. They would have work to do. Work that only they, the coalition of 1980 and 3042 could accomplish together.

There were people here in this world of 3042. How many or how few didn't matter. They were the nucleus, the beginnings of a future that would grow from 3042. They were the not-born, created in the laboratory. They would have to be taught about life. And love.

And other things that free men know...

THE END

If you've enjoyed this book, you will not want to miss these terrific titles…

ARMCHAIR SCI-FI & HORROR DOUBLE NOVELS, $12.95 each

D-31 **A HOAX IN TIME** by Keith Laumer
INSIDE EARTH by Poul Anderson

D-32 **TERROR STATION** by Dwight V. Swain
THE WEAPON FROM ETERNITY by Dwight V. Swain

D-33 **THE SHIP FROM INFINITY** by Edmond Hamilton
TAKEOFF by C. M. Kornbluth

D-34 **THE METAL DOOM** by David H. Keller
TWELVE TIMES ZERO by Howard Browne

D-35 **HUNTERS OUT OF SPACE** by Joseph Kelleam
INVASION FROM THE DEEP by Paul W. Fairman,

D-36 **THE BEES OF DEATH** by Robert Moore Williams
A PLAGUE OF PYTHONS by Frederik Pohl

D-37 **THE LORDS OF QUARMALL** by Fritz Leiber and Harry Fischer
BEACON TO ELSEWHERE by James H. Schmitz

D-38 **BEYOND PLUTO** by John S. Campbell
ARTERY OF FIRE by Thomas N. Scortia

D-39 **SPECIAL DELIVERY** by Kris Neville
NO TIME FOR TOFFEE by Charles F. Meyers

D-40 **JUNGLE IN THE SKY** by Milton Lesser
RECALLED TO LIFE by Robert Silverberg

ARMCHAIR SCIENCE FICTION CLASSICS, $12.95 each

C-10 **MARS IS MY DESTINATION**
by Frank Belknap Long

C-11 **SPACE PLAGUE**
by George O. Smith

C-12 **SO SHALL YE REAP**
by Rog Phillips

ARMCHAIR SCIENCE FICTION & HORROR GEMS SERIES, $12.95 each

G-3 **SCIENCE FICTION GEMS, Vol. Two**
James Blish and others

G-4 **HORROR GEMS, Vol. Two**
Joseph Payne Brennan and others

If you've enjoyed this book, you will not want to miss these terrific titles...

ARMCHAIR SCI-FI & HORROR DOUBLE NOVELS, $12.95 each

D-91 **THE TIME TRAP** by Henry Kuttner
THE LUNAR LICHEN by Hal Clement

D-92 **SARGASSO OF LOST STARSHIPS** by Poul Anderson
THE ICE QUEEN by Don Wilcox

D-93 **THE PRINCE OF SPACE** by Jack Williamson
POWER by Harl Vincent

D-94 **PLANET OF NO RETURN** by Howard Browne
THE ANNIHILATOR COMES by Ed Earl Repp

D-95 **THE SINISTER INVASION** by Edmond Hamilton
OPERATION TERROR by Murray Leinster

D-96 **TRANSIENT** by Ward Moore
THE WORLD-MOVER by George O. Smith

D-97 **FORTY DAYS HAS SEPTEMBER** by Milton Lesser
THE DEVIL'S PLANET by David Wright O'Brien

D-98 **THE CYBERENE** by Rog Phillips
BADGE OF INFAMY by Lester del Rey

D-99 **THE JUSTICE OF MARTIN BRAND** by Raymond A. Palmer
BRING BACK MY BRAIN by Dwight V. Swain

D-100 **WIDE-OPEN PLANET** by L. Sprague de Camp
AND THEN THE TOWN TOOK OFF by Richard Wilson

ARMCHAIR SCIENCE FICTION CLASSICS, $12.95 each

C-31 **THE GOLDEN GUARDSMEN**
by S. J. Byrne

C-32 **ONE AGAINST THE MOON**
by Donald A. Wollheim

C-33 **HIDDEN CITY**
by Chester S. Geier

ARMCHAIR SCIENCE FICTION & HORROR GEMS SERIES, $12.95 each

G-9 **SCIENCE FICTION GEMS, Vol. Five**
Clifford D. Simak and others

G-10 **HORROR GEMS, Vol. Five**
E. Hoffman Price and others

BEWARE THE DEADLY MARTIAN PLAGUE...

He was one of old Earth's outcasts, driven to share the wretched life of the Martian colonies—with nothing to live for, and only a dream to die for. Daniel Feldman was a doctor once. He made the mistake of saving a friend's life in violation of Medical Lobby rules. Now, he was a pariah, shunned by all, forbidden to touch another patient. But things were more loose on Mars. There, Doc Feldman was welcomed by the colonists, even as he was hunted by the authorities. But, when he discovered that a dreadful Martian plague might soon wipe out humanity on two planets, Feldman found himself a pivotal figure. War erupted. Earth was poised to utterly wipe out the Mars colony. A cure to the plague was the price of peace, and only Feldman could find it.

ABOUT LESTER DEL REY

Lester del Rey was born Leonard Knapp, in Saratoga, Minnesota, June 2, 1915. del Rey often told people that his real name was Ramon Felipe Alvarez-del Rey. He also claimed that his family was killed in a car accident in 1935. However, his sister has confirmed that his name was really Leonard Knapp and that the accident in 1935 killed his first wife but none of his parents, brother, and sister. He was an American science fiction author and editor. In his career, del Rey wrote over a hundred short stories and over two dozen novels, including the highly touted "Nerves" in 1956. He was the editor of such magazines as *Space Science Fiction, Science Fiction Adventures, Rocket Stories,* and a most successful line of Ballantine "del Rey" paperbacks starting in 1977. Some known pen names used by del Rey over the years were John Alvarez, Marion Henry, Philip James, Philip St. John, Charles Satterfield, and Erik van Lihn. In the 1950s, del Rey was one of the main authors writing science fiction for adolescents (along with Robert Heinlein and Andre Norton). He passed away at age 77 in New York City, on May 10th, 1993.

BADGE OF
INFAMY

By
LESTER DEL REY

ARMCHAIR FICTION
PO Box 4369, Medford, Oregon   97501-0168

*For more information about Armchair Books and products, visit our
website at…*

www.armchairfiction.com

Or email us at…

armchairfiction@yahoo.com

CHAPTER ONE
Pariah

The air of the city's cheapest flophouse was thick with the smells of harsh antiseptic and unwashed bodies. The early Christmas snowstorm had driven in every bum who could steal or beg the price of admission, and the long rows of cots were filled with fully clothed figures. Those who could afford the extra dime were huddled under thin, grimy blankets.

The pariah who had been Dr. Daniel Feldman enjoyed no such luxury. He tossed fitfully on a bare cot, bringing his face into the dim light. It had been a handsome face, but now the black stubble of beard lay over gaunt features and sunken cheeks. He looked ten years older than his scant thirty-two, and there were the beginnings of a snarl at the corners of his mouth. Clothes that had once been expensive were wrinkled and covered with grime that no amount of cleaning could remove. His tall, thin body was awkwardly curled up in a vain effort to conserve heat and one of his hands instinctively clutched at his tiny bag of possessions.

He stirred again, and suddenly jerked upright with a protest already forming on his lips. The ugly surroundings registered on his eyes, and he stared suspiciously at the other cots. But there was no sign that anyone had been trying to rob him of his bindle or the precious bag of cheap tobacco.

He started to relax back onto the couch when a sound caught his attention, even over the snoring of the others. It was a low wail, the sound of a man who can no longer control himself.

Feldman swung to the cot on his left as the moan hacked off. The man there was well fed and clean-shaven, but his face was gray with sickness. He was writhing and clutching his stomach, arching his back against the misery inside him.

"Space-stomach?" Feldman diagnosed.

He had no need of the weak answering nod. He'd treated such cases several times in the past. The disease was usually caused by the absence of gravity out in space, but it could be brought on later from abuse of the weakened internal organs, such as the intake of too much bad liquor. The man must have been frequenting the wrong space-front bars.

Now he was obviously dying. Violent peristaltic contractions seemed to be tearing the intestines out of him, and the paroxysms were coming faster. His eyes darted to Feldman's tobacco sack and there was animal appeal in them.

Feldman hesitated, then reluctantly rolled a smoke. He held the cigarette while the spaceman took a long, gasping drag on it. He smoked the remainder himself, letting the harsh tobacco burn against his lungs and sicken his empty stomach. Then he shrugged and threaded his way through the narrow aisles toward the attendant.

"Better get a doctor," he said bitterly, when the young punk looked up at him. "You've got a man dying of space-stomach on 214."

The sneer on the kid's face deepened. "Yeah? We don't pay for doctors every time some wino wants to throw up. Forget it and get back where you belong, bo."

"You'll have a corpse on your hands in an hour," Feldman insisted. "I know space-stomach, damn it."

The kid turned back to his lottery sheet. "Go treat yourself if you wanta play doctor. Go on, scram—before I toss you out in the snow!"

One of Feldman's white-knuckled hands reached for the attendant. Then he caught himself. He started to turn back, hesitated, and finally faced the kid again. "I'm not fooling.

And I *was* a doctor," he stated. "My name is Daniel Feldman."

The attendant nodded absently, until the words finally penetrated. He looked up, studied Feldman with surprised curiosity and growing contempt, and reached for the phone. "Gimme Medical Directory," he muttered.

Feldman felt the kid's eyes on his back as he stumbled through the aisles to his cot again. He slumped down, rolling another cigarette in hands that shook. The sick man was approaching delirium now, and the moans were mixed with weak whining sounds of fear. Other men had wakened and were watching, but nobody made a move to help.

The retching and writhing of the sick man had begun to weaken, but it was still not too late to save him. Hot water and skillful massage could interrupt the paroxysms. In fifteen minutes, Feldman could have stopped the attack completely.

He found his feet on the floor and his hands already reaching out. Savagely he pulled himself back. Sure, he could save the man—and wind up in the gas chamber! There'd be no mercy for his second offense against Lobby laws. If the spaceman lived, Feldman might get off with a flogging—that was standard punishment for a pariah who stepped out of line. But with his luck, there would be a heart arrest and another juicy story for the papers.

Idealism! The Medical Lobby made a lot out of the word. But it wasn't for him. A pariah had no business thinking of others.

As Feldman sat there staring, the spaceman grew quieter. Sometimes, even at this stage, massage could help. It was harder without liberal supplies of hot water, but the massage was the really important treatment. It was the trembling of Feldman's hands that stopped him. He no longer had the strength or the certainty to make the massage effective.

He was glaring at his hands in self-disgust when the legal doctor arrived. The man was old and tired. Probably he had been another idealist who had wound up defeated, content to leave things up to the established procedures of the Medical Lobby. He looked it as he bent over the dying man.

The doctor turned back at last to the attendant. "Too late. The best I can do is ease his pain. The call should have been made half an hour earlier."

He had obviously never handled space-stomach before. He administered a hypo that probably held narconal. Feldman watched, his guts tightening sympathetically for the shock that would be to the sick man. But at least it would shorten his sufferings. The final seizure lasted only a minute or so.

"Hopeless," the doctor said. His eyes were clouded for a moment, and then he shrugged. "Well, I'll make out a death certificate. Anyone here know his name?"

His eyes swung about the cots until they came to rest on Feldman. He frowned, and a twisted smile curved his lips.

"Feldman, isn't it? You still look something like your pictures. Do you know the deceased?"

Feldman shook his head bitterly. "No. I don't know his name. I don't even know why he wasn't cyanotic at the end, *if* it was space-stomach. Do you, doctor?"

The old man threw a startled glance at the corpse. Then he shrugged and nodded to the attendant. "Well, go through his things. If he still has a space ticket, I can get his name from that."

The kid began pawing through the bag that had fallen from the cot. He dragged out a pair of shoes, half a bottle of cheap rum, a wallet and a bronze space ticket. He wasn't quick enough with the wallet, and the doctor took it from him.

"Medical Lobby authorization. If he has any money, it covers my fee and the rest goes to his own Lobby." There were several bills, all of large denominations. He turned the ticket over and began filling in the death certificate. "Arthur Billings. Space Lobby. Crewman. Cause of death, idiopathic gastroenteritis *and* delirium tremens."

There had been no evidence of delirium tremens, but apparently the doctor felt he had scored a point. He tossed the space ticket toward the shoes, closed his bag, and prepared to leave.

"Hey, doc!" The attendant's voice was indignant. "Hey, what about my reporting fee?"

The doctor stopped. He glanced at the kid, then toward Feldman, his face a mixture of speculation and dislike. He took a dollar bill from the wallet. "That's right," he admitted. "The fee for reporting a solvent case. Medical Lobby rules apply—even to a man who breaks them."

The kid's hand was out, but the doctor dropped the dollar onto Feldman's cot. "There's your fee, pariah." He left, forcing the protesting attendant to precede him.

Feldman reached for the bill. It was blood money for letting a man die—but it meant cigarettes and food—or shelter for another night, if he could get a mission meal. He no longer could afford pride. Grimly, he pocketed the bill, staring at the face of the dead man. It looked back sightlessly, now showing a faint speckling of tiny dots. They caught Feldman's eyes, and he bent closer. There should be no black dots on the skin of a man who died of space-stomach. And there should have been cyanosis…

He swore and bent down to find the wrecks of his shoes. He couldn't worry about anything now but getting away from here before the attendant made trouble. His eyes rested on the shoes of the dead man—sturdy boots that would last for another year. They could do the corpse no good; someone else would steal them if he didn't. But he hesitated, cursing himself.

The right boot fitted better than he could have expected, but something got in the way as he tried to put the left one on. His fingers found the bronze ticket. He turned it over, considering it. He wasn't ready to fraud his identity for what he'd heard of life on the spaceships, yet. But he shoved it into his pocket and finished lacing the boots.

Outside, the snow was still falling, but it had turned to slush, and the sidewalk was soggy underfoot. There was going to be no work shoveling snow, he realized. This would melt before the day was over. Feldman hunched the suitcoat up, shivering as the cold bit into him. The boots felt good, though; if he'd had socks, they would have been completely comfortable.

He passed a cheap restaurant, and the smell of the synthetics set his stomach churning. It had been two days since his last real meal, and the dollar burned in his pocket. But he had to wait. There was a fair chance this early that he could scavenge something edible.

He shuffled on. After a while, the cold bothered him less, and he passed through the hunger spell. He rolled another smoke and sucked at it, hardly thinking. It was better that way.

It was much later when the big caduceus set into the sidewalk snapped him back to awareness of where he'd traveled. His undirected feet had led him much too far uptown, following old habits. This was the Medical Lobby building, where he'd spent more than enough time, including three weeks in custody before they stripped him of all rank and status.

His eyes wandered to the ornate entrance where he'd first emerged as a pariah. He'd meant to walk down those steps as if he were still a man. But each step had drained his resolution, until he'd finally covered his face and slunk off, knowing himself for what the world had branded him.

He stood there now, staring at the smug young medical politicians and the tired old general practitioners filing in and out. One of the latter halted, fumbled in his pocket and drew out a quarter.

"Merry Christmas!" he said dully.

Feldman fingered the coin. Then he saw a gray Medical policeman watching him, and he knew it was time to move on. Sooner or later, someone would recognize him here.

He clutched the quarter and turned to look for a coffee shop that sold the synthetics to which his metabolism had been switched. No shop would serve him here, but he could buy coffee and a piece of cake to take out.

A flurry of motion registered from the corner of his eye, and he glanced back.

"Taxi! Taxi!"

The girl rushing down the steps had a clear soprano voice, cultured and commanding. The gray Medical uniform seemed molded to her shapely figure and her red hair glistened in the lights of the street. Her snub nose and determined mouth weren't the current fashion, but nobody stopped to think of fashions when they saw her. She didn't have to be the daughter of the president of Medical Lobby to rule.

It was Chris—Chris Feldman once, and now Chris Ryan again.

Feldman swung toward a cab. For a moment, his attitude was automatic and assured, and the cab stopped before the driver noticed his clothes. He picked up the bag Chris dropped and swung it onto the front seat. She was fumbling in her change purse as he turned back to shut the door.

"Thank you, my good man," she said. She could be gracious, even to a pariah, when his homage suited her. She dropped two quarters into his hand, raising her eyes.

Recognition flowed into them, followed by icy shock. She yanked the cab door shut and shouted something to the driver. The cab took off with a rush that left Feldman in a backwash of slush and mud.

He glanced down at the coins in his hand. It was his lucky day, he thought bitterly.

He moved across the street and away, not bothering about the squeal of brakes and the honking horns. He looked back only once, toward the glowing sign that topped the building. *Your health is our business!* Then the great symbol of the health business faded behind him, and he stumbled on, sucking incessantly at the cigarettes he rolled. One hand clutched the bronze badge belonging to the dead man and his stolen boots drove onward through the melting snow.

It was Christmas in the year 2100 on the protectorate of Earth

CHAPTER TWO
Lobby

Feldman had set his legs the problem of heading for the great spaceport and escape from Earth, and he let them take him without further guidance. His mind was wrapped up in a whirl of the past—his past and that of the whole planet. Both pasts had in common the growth and sudden ruin of idealism.

Idealism! Throughout history, some men had sought the ideal, and most had called it freedom. Only fools expected absolute freedom, but wise men dreamed up many systems of relative freedom, including democracy. They had tried that in America, as the last fling of the dream. It had been a good attempt, too.

The men who drew the Constitution had been pretty practical dreamers. They came to their task after a bitter war and a worse period of wild chaos, and they had learned where idealism stopped and idiocy began. They set up a republic with all the elements of democracy that they considered safe. It had worked well enough to make America the number one power of the world. But the men who followed the framers of the new plan were a different sort, without the knowledge of practical limits.

The privileges their ancestors had earned in blood and care became automatic rights. Practical men tried to explain that there were no such rights—that each generation had to pay for its rights with responsibility. That kind of talk didn't get far. People wanted to hear about rights, not about duties.

They took the phrase that all men were created equal and left out the implied kicker that equality was in the sight of

God and before the law. They wanted an equality with the greatest men without giving up their drive toward mediocrity, and they meant to have it. In a way, they got it.

They got the vote extended to everyone. The man on subsidy or public dole could vote to demand more. The man who read of nothing beyond sex crimes could vote on the great political issues of the world. No ability was needed for his vote. In fact, he was assured that voting alone was enough to make him a fine and noble citizen. He loved that, if he bothered to vote at all that year. He became a great man by listing his unthought, hungry desire for someone to take care of him without responsibility. So he went out and voted for the man who promised him most, or who looked most like what his limited dreams felt to be a father image or son image or hero image. He never bothered later to see how the men he'd elected had handled the jobs he had given them.

Someone had to look, of course, and someone did. Organized special interests stepped in where the mob had failed. Lobbies grew up. There had always been pressure groups, but now they developed into a third arm of the government.

The old Farm Lobby was unbeatable. The big farmers shaped the laws they wanted. They convinced the little farmers it was for the good of all, and they made the story stick well enough to swing the farm vote. They made the laws when it came to food and crops.

The last of the great lobbies was Space, probably. It was an accident that grew up so fast it never even knew it wasn't a real part of the government. It developed during a period of chaos when another country called Russia got the first hunk of metal above the atmosphere and when the representatives who had been picked for everything but their grasp of science and government went into panic over a myth of national prestige.

The space effort was turned over to the aircraft industry, which had never been able to manage itself successfully except under the stimulus of war or a threat of war. The failing airplane industry became the space combine overnight, and nobody kept track of how big it was, except a few sharp operators.

They worked out a system of subcontracts that spread the profits so wide that hardly a company of any size in the country wasn't getting a share. Thus a lot of patriotic, noble voters got their pay from companies in the lobby block and could be panicked by the lobby at the first mention of recession.

So Space Lobby took over completely in its own field. It developed enough pressure to get whatever appropriations it wanted, even over Presidential veto. It created the only space experts, which meant that the men placed in government agencies to regulate it came from its own ranks.

The other lobbies learned a lot from Space.

There had been a medical lobby long before, but it had been a conservative group, mostly concerned with protecting medical autonomy and ethics. It also tried to prevent government control of treatment and payment, feeling that it couldn't trust the people to know where to stop. But its history was a long series of retreats.

It fought what it called socialized medicine. But the people wanted their troubles handled free—which meant by government spending, since that could be added to the national debt, and thus didn't seem to cost anything. It lost, and eventually the government paid most medical costs, with doctors working on a fixed fee. Then quantity of treatment paid, rather than quality. Competence no longer mattered so much. The Lobby lost, but didn't know it—because the lowered standards of competence in the profession lowered the caliber of men running the political aspects of that profession as exemplified by the Lobby.

It took a world-wide plague to turn the tide. The plague began in old China; anything could start there, with more than a billion people huddled in one area and a few madmen planning to conquer the world. It might have been a laboratory mutation, but nobody could ever prove it.

It wiped out two billion people, depopulated Africa and most of Asia, and wrecked Europe, leaving only America comparatively safe to take over. An obscure scientist in one of the laboratories run by the Medical Lobby found a cure before the first waves of the epidemic hit America. Rutherford Ryan, then head of the Lobby, made sure that Medical Lobby got all the credit.

By the time the world recovered, America ran it and the Medical Lobby was untouchable. Ryan made a deal with Space Lobby, and the two effectively ran the world. None of the smaller lobbies could buck them, and neither could the government.

There was still a president and a congress, as there had been a Senate under the Roman Caesars. But the two Lobbies ran themselves as they chose. The real government had become a kind of oligarchy, as it always did after too much false democracy ruined the ideals of real and practical self-rule. A man belonged to his Lobby, just as a serf had belonged to his feudal landlord.

It was a safe world now. Maybe progress had been halted at about the level of 1980, but so long as the citizens didn't break the rules of their lobbies, they had very little to worry about. For that, for security and the right not to think, most people were willing to leave well enough alone.

Some rules seemed harsh, of course, such as the law that all operations had to be performed in Lobby hospitals. But that could be justified; it was the only safe kind of surgery and the only way to make sure there was no unsupervised experimentation, such as that which supposedly caused the plague. The rule was now an absolute ethic of medicine. It also made for better fees.

Feldman's father had stuck by the rule but had questioned it. Feldman learned not to question in medical school. He scored second in Medical Ethics only to Christina Ryan.

He had never figured why she singled him out for her attentions, but he gloried in both those attentions and the results. He became automatically a rising young man, the favorite of the daughter of the Lobby president. He went through internship without a sign of trouble. Chris humored him in his desire to spend three years of practice in a poor section loaded with disease, and her father approved; such selfless dedication was the perfect image projection for a future son-in-law. In return, he agreed to follow that period by becoming an administrator. A doctor's doctor, as they put it.

They were married in April and his office was ready in May, complete with a staff of eighty. The publicity releases had gone out, and the Public Relations Lobby that handled news and education was paid to begin the greatest build-up any young genius ever had.

They celebrated that, with a little party of some four hundred people and reporters at Ryan's lodge in Canada. It was to be a gala weekend.

It was then that Baxter shot himself.

Baxter had been Feldman's closest friend in the Lobby. He'd come along to handle press relations and had gotten romantic about the countryside, never having been out of a city before. He hired a guide and went hunting, eighty miles beyond the last outpost of civilization. Somehow, he got his hand on a gun, though only guides were supposed to touch them, managed to overcome its safety devices, and then pulled the trigger with the gun pointed the wrong way.

Chris, Feldman and Harnett from Public Relations had accompanied him on the trip. They were sitting in a nearby car while Feldman enjoyed the scenery, Chris made further plans, and Harnett gathered material. There was also a photographer and writer, but they hadn't been introduced by name.

Feldman reached Baxter first. The man was moaning and scared, and he was bleeding profusely. Only a miracle had saved him from instant death. The bullet had struck a rib, been deflected and robbed of some of its energy, and had barely reached the heart. But it had pierced the pericardium, as best Feldman could guess, and it could be fatal at any moment.

He'd reached for a probe without thinking. Chris knocked his hand aside.

She was right, of course. He couldn't operate outside a hospital. But they had no phone in the lodge where the guide lived and no way to summon an ambulance. They'd have to drive Baxter back in the car, which would almost certainly result in his death.

When Feldman seemed uncertain, Harnett had given his warning in a low but vehement voice. "You touch him, Dan, and I'll spread it in every one of our media. I'll have to. It's the only way to retain public confidence. There'd be a leak, with all the guides and others here, and we can't afford that. I like you—you have color. But touch that wound and I'll crucify you."

Chris added her own threats. She'd spent years making him the outlet for all her ambitions, denied because women were still only second-rate members of Medical Lobby. She couldn't let it go now. And she was probably genuinely shocked.

Baxter groaned again and started to bleed more profusely.

There wasn't much equipment. Feldman operated with a pocketknife sterilized in a bottle of expensive Scotch and only anodyne tablets in place of anesthesia. He got the bullet out and sewed up the wound with a bit of surgical thread he'd been using to tie up a torn good-luck emblem. The photographer and writer recorded the whole thing. Chris swore harshly and beat her fists against the bole of a tree. But Baxter lived. He recovered completely, and was shocked at the heinous thing that had been done to him.

They crucified Feldman.

CHAPTER THREE
Spaceman

Most crewmen lived rough, ugly lives—and usually, short ones. Passengers and officers on the big tubs were given the equivalent of gravity in spinning compartments, but the crews rode "free". The lucky crewmen lived through their accidents, got space-stomach now and then, and recovered. Nobody cared about the others.

Feldman's ticket was work-stamped for the *Navaho*, and nobody questioned his identity. He suffered through the agony of acceleration on the shuttle up to the orbital station, then was sick as acceleration stopped. But he was able to control himself enough to follow other crewmen down a hall of the station toward the *Navaho*. The big ships never touched a planet, always docking at the stations.

A checker met the crew and reached for their badges. He barely glanced at them, punched a mark for each on his checkoff sheet, and handed them back. "Deckmen forward, tubemen to the rear," he ordered. "*Navaho* blasts in fifteen minutes. Hey, you! You're tubes."

Feldman grunted. He should have expected it. Tubemen had the lowest lot of all the crew. Between the killing work, the heat of the tubes, and occasional doses of radiation, their lives weren't worth the metal value of their tickets.

He began pulling himself clumsily along a shaft, dodging freight the loaders were tossing from hand to hand. A bag hit his head, drawing blood, and another caught him in the groin.

"Watch it, bo," a loader yelled at him. "You dent that bag and they'll brig you. Cantcha see it's got a special courtesy stripe?"

It had a brilliant green stripe, he saw. It also had a name, printed in block letters that shouted their identity before he could read the words. *Dr. Christina Ryan, Southport, Mars.*

And he'd had to choose this time to leave Earth!

Suddenly he was glad he was assigned to the tubes. It was the one place on the ship where he'd be least likely to run into her. As a doctor and a courtesy passenger, she'd have complete run of the ship, but she'd hardly bother with the dangerous and unpleasant tube section.

He dragged his way back, beginning to sweat with the effort. The *Navaho* was an old ship. A lot of the handholds were missing, and he had to throw himself along by erratic leaps. He was gaining proficiency, but not enough to handle himself if the ship blasted off. Time was growing short when he reached the aft bunkroom where the other tubemen were waiting.

"Ben," one husky introduced himself. "Tube chief. Know how to work this?"

Feldman could see that they were assembling a small still. He'd heard of the phenomenal quantities of beer spacemen drank, and now he realized what really happened to it. Hard liquor was supposed to be forbidden, but they made their own. "I can work it," he decided. "I'm—uh—Dan."

"Okay, Dan." Ben glanced at the clock. "Hit the sacks, boys."

By the time Feldman could settle into the sacklike hammock, the *Navaho* began to shake faintly, and weight piled up. It was mild compared to that on the shuttle, since the big ships couldn't take high acceleration. Space had been conquered for more than a century, but the ships were still flimsy tubs that took months to reach Mars, using immense amounts of fuel. Only the valuable plant hormones from Mars made commerce possible at the ridiculously high freight rate.

Three hours later he began to find out why spacemen didn't seem to fear dying or turning pariah. The tube quarters had grown insufferably hot during the long blast, but the main tube-room was blistering as Ben led the men into it. The chief handed out spacesuits and motioned for Dan.

"Greenhorn, aincha? Okay, I'll take you with me. We go out in the tubes and pull the lining. I pry up the stuff, you carry it back here and stack it."

They sealed off the tube-room, pumped out the air, and went into the steaming, mildly radioactive tubes, just big enough for a man on hands and knees. Beyond the tube mouth was empty space, waiting for the man who slipped. Ben began ripping out the eroded blocks with a special tool. Feldman carried them back and stacked them along with others. A plasma furnace melted them down into new blocks. The work grew progressively worse as the distance to the tube-room increased. The tube mouth yawned closer and closer. There were no handholds there—only the friction of a man's body in the tube.

Life settled into a dull routine of labor, sleep, and the brief relief of the crude white mule from the still.

They were six weeks out and almost finished with the tube cleaning when Number Two tube blew. Bits of the remaining radioactive fuel must have collected slowly until they reached blow-point. Feldman in Number One would have gone sailing out into space, but Ben reacted at once. As the ship leaped slightly, Feldman brought up sharply against the chief's braced body. For a second their fate hung in the balance. Then it was over, and Ben shoved him back, grinning faintly.

He jerked his thumb and touched helmets briefly. "There they go, Dan."

The two men who had been working in Number Two were charred lumps, drifting out into space.

No further comment was made on it, except that they'd have to work harder from now on, since they were shorthanded.

That rest period Feldman came down with a mild attack of space-stomach—which meant no more drinking for him—and was off work for a day. Then the pace picked up. The tubes were cleared and they began laying the new lining for the landing blasts. There was no time for thought after that. Mars' orbital station lay close when the work was finished.

Ben slapped Feldman on the back. "Ya ain't bad for a greenie, Dan. We all get six-day passes on Mars. Hit the sack now so you won't waste time sleeping then. We'll hear it when the ship berths."

Feldman didn't hear it, but the others did. He felt Ben shaking his shoulder, trying to drag him out of the sack. "Grab your junk, Dan."

Ben picked up Feldman's nearly empty bag and tossed it toward him, before his eyes were fully open. He grabbed for it and missed. He grabbed again, with Ben's laughter in his ears. The bag hit the wall and fell open, spilling its contents.

Feldman began gathering it up, but the chief was no longer laughing. A big hand grabbed up the space ticket suddenly, and there was no friendliness now on Ben's face.

"Art Billing's card!" Ben told the other tubemen. "Five trips I made with Art. He was saving his money, going to buy a farm on Mars. Five trips and one more to go before he had enough. Now you show up with his ticket!"

The tubemen moved forward toward Feldman. There was no indecision. To them, apparently, trial had been held and sentence passed.

"Wait a minute," Feldman began. "Billings died of—"

A fist snaked past his raised hand and connected with his jaw. He bounced off a wall. A wrench sailed toward him, glanced off his arm, and ripped at his muscles. Another heavy fist struck.

Abruptly, Ben's voice cut through their yells. "Hold it!" He shoved through the group, tossing men backwards. "Stow it! We can take care of him later. Right now, this is captain's business. You fools want to lose your leave?" He indicated two of the others. "You two bring him along—and keep him quiet!"

The two grabbed Feldman's arms and dragged him along as the chief began pulling his way forward through the tubes up towards the control section of the ship. Feldman took a quick glance at their faces and made no effort to resist; they obviously would have enjoyed any chance to subdue him.

They were stopped twice by minor officers, then sent on. They finally found the captain near the exit lock, apparently assisting the passengers to leave. Most of them went on into the shuttle, but Chris Ryan remained behind as the captain listened to Ben's report and inspected the false ticket.

Finally the captain turned to Feldman. "You. What's your name?"

Chris' eyes were squarely on Feldman, cold and furious. "He *was* Doctor Daniel Feldman, Captain Marker," she stated.

Feldman stood paralyzed. He'd been unwilling to face Chris. He wanted to avoid all the past. But the idea that she would denounce him had never entered his head. There was no Medical rule involved. She knew that as a pariah he was forbidden to board a passenger ship, of course. But she'd been his wife once!

Marker bowed slightly to her. "Thank you, Dr. Ryan. I should take this criminal back to Earth in chains, I suppose. But he's hardly worth the freightage. You men. Want to take him down to Mars and ground him there?"

Ben grinned and touched his forelock. "Thank you, sir. We'd enjoy that."

"Good. His pay reverts to the ship's fund. That's all, men."

Feldman started to protest, but a fist lashed savagely against his mouth.

He made no other protests as they dragged him into the crew shuttle that took off for Southport. He avoided their eyes and sat hunched over. It was Ben who finally broke the silence.

"What happened to Art's money? He had a pile on him."

"Go to hell!"

"Give, I said!" Ben twisted his arm back toward his shoulder, applying increasing pressure.

"A doctor took it for his fee when Billings died of space-stomach. Damn you, I couldn't help him!"

Ben looked at the others. "Med Lobby fee, eh? All the market will take. Umm. It could be, maybe." He shrugged. "Okay, reasonable doubt. We won't kill you, bo. Not quite, we won't."

The shuttle landed and Ben handed out the little helmets and aspirators that made life possible in Mars' thin air. Outside, the tubemen took turns holding Feldman and beating him while the passengers disembarked from their shuttle. As he slumped into unconsciousness, he had a picture of Chris Ryan's frozen face as she moved steadily toward the port station.

CHAPTER FOUR
Martian

It was night when Feldman came to, and the temperature was dropping rapidly. He struggled to sit up through a fog of pain. Somewhere in his bag, he should have an anodyne tablet that would kill any ache. He finally found the pill and swallowed it, fumbling with the aspirator lip opening.

The aspirator meant life to him now, he suddenly realized. He twisted to stare at the tiny charge-indicator for the battery. It showed half-charge. Then he saw that someone had attached another battery beside it. He puzzled briefly over it, but his immediate concern was for shelter.

Apparently he was still where he had been knocked out. There was a light coming from the little station, and he headed toward that, fumbling for the few quarters that represented his entire fortune.

Maybe it would have been better if the tubemen had killed him. Batteries were an absolute necessity here, food and shelter would be expensive, and he had no skills to earn his way. At most, he had only a day or so left. But meantime, he had to find warmth before the cold killed him.

The tiny restaurant in the station was still open, and the air was warm inside. He pulled off the aspirator, shutting off the battery.

The counterman didn't even glance up as he entered. Feldman gazed at the printed menu and flinched.

"Soup," he ordered. It was the cheapest item he could find.

The counterman stared at him, obviously spotting his Earth origin. "You adjusted to synthetics?"

Feldman nodded. Earth operated on a mixed diet, with synthetics for all who couldn't afford the natural foods there. But Mars was all synthetic. Many of the chemicals in food could exist in either of two forms, or isomers; they were chemically alike, but differently crystallized. Sometimes either form was digestible, but frequently the body could use only the isomer to which it was adjusted.

Martian plants produced different isomers from those on Earth. Since the synthetic foods turned out to be Mars-normal, that was probably the more natural form. Research designed to let the early colonists live off native food here had turned up an enzyme that enabled the body to handle either isomer. In a few weeks of eating Martian or synthetic food, the body adapted; without more enzyme, it lost its power to handle Earth-normal food.

The cheapness of synthetics and the discovery that many diseases common to Earth would not attack Mars-normal bodies led to the wide use of synthetics on Earth. No pariah could have been expected to afford Earth-normal.

Feldman finished the soup, and found a cigarette that was smokable. "Any objections if I sit in the waiting room?"

He'd expected a rejection, but the counterman only shrugged. The waiting room was almost dark and the air was chilly, but there was normal pressure. He found a bench and slumped onto it, lighting his cigarette. He'd miss the smokes—but probably not for long. He finished the cigarette reluctantly and sat huddled on the bench, waiting for morning.

The airlock opened later, and feet sounded on the boards of the waiting-room floor, but he didn't look up until a thin beam of light hit him. Then he sighed and nodded. The shoes, made of some odd fiber, didn't look like those of a cop, but this was Mars. He could see only a hulking shadow behind the light.

"You the man who was a medical doctor?" The voice was dry and old.

"Yeah," Feldman answered. "Once."

"Good. Thought that space crewman was just lying drunk at first. Come along, Doc."

"Why?" It didn't matter, but if they wanted him to move on, they'd have to push a little harder.

The light swung up to show the other. He was the shade of old leather with a bleached patch of sandy hair and the deepest gray eyes Feldman had ever seen. It was a face that could have belonged to a country storekeeper in New England, with the same hint of dry humor. The man was dressed in padded levis and a leather jacket of unguessable age. His aspirator seemed worn and patched, and one big hand fumbled with it.

"Because we're friends, Doc," the voice drawled at him. "Because you might as well come with us as sit here. Maybe we have a job for you."

Feldman shrugged and stood up. If the man was a Lobby policeman, he was different from the usual kind. Nothing could be worse than the present prospects.

They went out through the doors of the waiting room toward a rattletrap vehicle. It looked something like a cross between a schoolboy's jalopy and a scaled-down army tank of former times. The treads were caterpillar style, and the stubby body was completely enclosed. A tiny airlock stuck out from the rear.

Two men were inside, both bearded. The old man grinned at them. "Mark, Lou, meet Doc Feldman. Sit, Doc. I'm Jake Mullens, and you might say we were farmers."

The motor started with a wheeze. The tractor swung about and began heading away from Southport toward the desert dunes. It shook and rattled, but it seemed to make good time.

"I don't know anything about farming," Feldman protested.

Jake shrugged. "No, of course not. Couple of our friends heard about you where a spaceman was getting drunk and tipped us off. We know who you are. Here, try a bracky?"

Feldman took what seemed to be a cigarette and studied it doubtfully. It was coarse and fibrous inside, with a thin, hard shell that seemed to be a natural growth, as if it had been chopped from some vine. He lighted it, not knowing what to expect. Then he coughed as the bitter, rancid smoke burned at his throat. He started to throw it down, and hesitated. Jake was smoking one, and it had killed the craving for tobacco almost instantly.

"Some like 'em, most don't," Jake said. "They won't hurt you. Look—see that? Old Martian ruins. Built by some race a million years ago. Only half a dozen on Mars."

It was only a clump of weathered stone buildings in the light from the tractor, and Feldman had seen better in the stereo shots. It was interesting only because it connected with the legendary Martian race, like the canals that showed from space but could not be seen on the surface of the planet.

Feldman waited for the other to go on, but Jake was silent. Finally, he ground out the butt of the weed. "Okay, Jake. What do you want with me?"

"Consultation, maybe. Ever hear of herb doctors? I'm one of them."

Feldman knew that the Lobby permitted some leniency here, due to the scarcity of real medical help. There was only one decent hospital at Northport, on the opposite side of the planet.

Jake sighed and reached for another bracky weed. "Yeah, I'm pretty good with herbs. But I got a sick village on my hands and I can't handle it. We can't all mortgage our work to pay for a trip to Northport. Southport's all messed up while the new she-doctor gets her metabolism changed. Maybe the old guy there would have helped, but he died a couple months ago. So it looks like you're our only hope."

"Then you have no hope," Feldman told him sickly. "I'm a pariah, Jake. I can't do a thing for you."

"We heard about your argument with the Lobby. News reaches Mars. But these are mighty sick people, Doc."

Feldman shook his head. "Better take me back. I'm not allowed to practice medicine. The charge would be first-degree murder if anything happened."

Lou leaned forward. "Shall I talk to him, Jake?"

The old man grimaced. "Time enough. Let him see what we got first."

Sand howled against the windshield and the tractor bumped and surged along. Feldman took another of the weeds and tried to estimate their course. But he had no idea where they were when the tractor finally stopped. There was a village of small huts that seemed to be merely entrances to living quarters dug under the surface. They led him into one and through a tunnel into a large room filled with simple cots and the unhappy sounds of sick people.

Two women were disconsolately trying to attend to the half-dozen sick—four children and two adults. Their faces brightened as they saw Jake, then fell. "Eb and Tilda died," they reported.

Feldman looked at the two figures under the sheets and whistled. The same black specks he had seen on the face of Billings covered the skins of the two old people who had died.

"Funny," Jake said slowly. "They didn't quite act like the others and they sure died mighty fast. Darn it, I had it figured for that stuff in the book. Infantile paralysis. How about it, Doc? Sort of like a cold, stiff sore neck."

It was clearly polio—one of the diseases that could attack Mars-normal flesh. Feldman nodded at the symptoms, staring at the sick kids. He shrugged, finally. "There's a cure for it, but I don't have the serum. Neither do you, or you wouldn't have brought me here. I couldn't help if I wanted to."

"That old book didn't list a cure," Jake told him. "But it said the kids didn't have to be crippled. There was something about a Kenny treatment. Doc, does the stuff really cripple for life?"

Feldman saw one of the boys flinch. He dropped his eyes, remembering the Lobby's efficient spy service on Earth and wondering what it was like here. But he knew the outcome.

"Damn you, Jake!"

Jake chuckled. "Thought you would. We sure appreciate it. Just tell us what to do, Doc."

Feldman began writing down his requirements, trying to remember the details of the treatment. Exercise, hot compresses, massage. It was coming back to him. He'd have to do it himself, of course, to get the feel of it. He couldn't explain it well enough. But he couldn't turn his back on the kids, either.

"Maybe I can help," he said doubtfully as he moved toward a cot.

"No, Doc." Jake's voice wasn't amused any longer, and he held the younger man back. "You're doing us a favor, and I'll be darned if I'll let you stick your neck out too far. You can't treat 'em yourself. Mars is tougher than Earth. You should live under Space Lobby *and* Medical Lobby here a while. Oh, maybe they don't mind a few fools like me being herb doctors, but they'd sure hate to have a man who can do real medicine outside their hands. You let me do it, or get in the tractor and I'll have Lou drive you back. Once you start in here, there'll be no stopping. Believe me."

Feldman looked at him, seeing the colonials around him for the first time as people. It had been a long time since he'd been treated as a fellow human by anyone.

Jake was right, he knew. Once he put his hand to the bandage, eventually there'd be no turning back from the scalpel. These people needed medical help too desperately. Eventually, the news would spread, and the Lobby police would come for him. Chris couldn't afford to shield him. In fact, he was sure now that she'd hunt him night and day.

"Don't be a fool, Jake," he ordered brusquely. He handed his list to one of the women. "You'll have to learn to do what I do," he told the people there. "You'll have to work like fools for weeks. But there won't be many crippled children. I can promise that much!"

He blinked sharply at the sudden hope in their eyes. But his mind went on wondering how long it would be before the inevitable would catch up with him. With luck, maybe a few months. But he hadn't been blessed with any superabundance of luck. It would probably be less time than he thought.

CHAPTER FIVE
Surgery

Doc Feldman's luck was better than he had expected. For an Earth year, he was a doctor again, moving about from village to village as he was needed and doing what he could.

The village had been isolated during the early colonization when Mars made a feeble attempt to break free of Space Lobby. Their supplies had been cut off and they had been forced to do for themselves. Now they were largely self-sufficient. They grew native plants and extracted hormones in crude little chemical plants. The hormones were traded to the big chemical plants for a pittance to buy what had to come from Earth. Other jury-rigged affairs synthesized much of their food. But mostly they learned to get along on what Mars provided.

Doc Feldman learned from them. Money was no longer part of his life. He ate with whatever family needed him and slipped into the life around him.

He was learning Martian medicine and finding that his Earth courses were mostly useless. No wonder the villagers distrusted Lobby doctors. Doc had his own little laboratory where he had managed to start making Mars-normal penicillin—a primitive antibiotic, but better than nothing.

Jake had come to remind him that it was his first anniversary, and now they were smoking bracky together.

"Sheer luck, Jake," Doc repeated. "You Martians are tough. But some day someone is going to die under my care, with the little equipment I have. Then—"

Jake nodded slowly. "Maybe, Doc. And maybe some day Mars will break free of the Lobbies. You'd better pray for that."

"I've been—" Doc stopped, realizing what he'd started to say. The old man chuckled.

"You've been talking rebellion for months, Doc. I hear rumors. Whenever you get mad, you want us to secede. But you don't really mean it yet. You can't picture any government but the one you're used to."

Doc grinned. Jake had a point, but it was not as strong as it would have been a few months before. The towns under the Lobby were cheap imitations of Earth, but here, divorced to a large extent from the lobbies, the villages were making Mars their own. Their ways might be strange; but they worked.

Jake shifted his body in the weak sunlight. "Newton village forgot to report a death on time. I hear Ryan is sweating them out, trying to prove it was your fault."

There was no evidence against him yet, Doc was sure. But Chris was out to prove something, and to get a reputation as a top-flight administrator. It must have hurt when they shipped her here as head of the lesser hemisphere of Mars. She'd expected to use Feldman as a front while she became the actual ruler of the whole Lobby. Now she wanted to strike back.

"She's using blackmail," he said, and some of his old bitterness was in his voice. "Anyone taking treatment from an herb doctor in this section is cut off from Medical Lobby service. Damn it, Jake, that could mean letting people die!"

"Yeah." Jake sighed softly. "It could mean letting people begin to think about getting rid of the Lobby, too. Well, I gotta help harvest the bracky. Take it easy on operating for a while, will you, Doc?"

"All right, Jake. But stop keeping the serious cases a secret. Two men died last month because you wouldn't call me for surgery. I've broken all my oaths already. It doesn't matter anymore."

"It matters, boy. We've been lucky, but some day one case will go to the hospital and they'll find your former work. Then they'll really be after you. The less you do the better."

Doc watched Jake slump off, then turned down into the little root cellar and back toward the room concealed behind it, where his crude laboratory lay. For the moment, he was free to work on the mystery of the black spots.

He kept running into them—always on the body of someone who died of something that seemed like a normal disease. Without a microscope, he was almost helpless, but he had taken specimens and tried to culture them. Some of his cultures had grown, though they might be nothing but unknown Martian fungi or bacteria. Mars was dry and almost devoid of air, but plants and a few smaller insects had survived and adapted. It wasn't by any means lifeless.

Without a microscope, he could do little but depend on his files of cases. But today there was new evidence. A villager had filched an Earth *Medical Journal* from the tractor driven by Chris Ryan and forwarded it to him. He found the black specks mentioned in a single paragraph, under skin diseases. Investigation of the diet was being made, since all cases were among people eating synthetics.

There was another article on aberrant cases—a few strange little misbehaviors in classical syndromes. He studied that, wondering. It had to be the same thing. Diet didn't account for the fact that the specks appeared only when the patient was near death.

Nor did it account for the hard lump at the base of the neck which he found in every case he could check. That might be coincidence, but he doubted it.

Whatever it was, it aggravated any other disease the patient had and made seemingly simple diseases turn out to be completely and rapidly fatal. Once syphilis had been called "The Great Imitator". This gave promise of being worse.

He shook his head, cursing his lack of equipment. Each month more people were dying with these specks—and he was helpless.

The concealed door broke open suddenly and a boy thrust his head in. "Doc, there's a man here from Einstein. Says his wife's dying."

The man was already coming into the room.

"She's powerful sick, Doc. Had a bellyache, fever, began throwing up. Pains under her belly, like she's had before. But this time it's awful."

Doc shot a few questions at him, frowning at what he heard. Then he began packing the few things that might help. There should be no appendicitis on Mars. The bugs responsible for that shouldn't have adapted to Mars-normal. But more and more infections found ways to cross the border. Gangrene had been able to get by without change, it seemed. So far, none of the contagious infections except polio and the common cold had made the jump.

This sounded like an advanced case, perhaps already involving peritonitis.

So far, he'd been lucky with penicillin, but each time he used it with grave doubts of its action on the Mars-adapted patients. If the appendix had burst, however, it was the only possible treatment.

He riffled through his stores; There was ether enough, fortunately. The villagers had made that for him out of Martian plants, using their complicated fermentation processes. He yelled for Jake, and the boy brought the old man back a moment later.

"Jake, I'll need more of that narcotic stuff. I don't want the woman writhing and tearing her stitches after the ether wears off."

"Can't get it, Doc." Jake's eyes seemed to cloud as he said it. "Distilling plant broke down. Doc, I don't like this case. That woman's been to the hospital three times. I hear she just got out recently. This might be a plant, or they figure they can't help her."

"They're afraid to try anything on Mars-normal flesh. They can't be proved wrong if they do nothing." Doc finished packing his bag and got ready to go out. "Jake, either I'm a doctor or I'm not. I can't worry when a woman may be dying."

For a second, Jake's expression was stubborn. Then the little crow's feet around his eyes deepened and the dry chuckle was back in his voice. "Right, Dr. Feldman." He flipped up his thumb and went off at a shuffling run toward the tractor. Lou and the man from Einstein followed Doc into the machine.

It was a silent ride, except for Doc's questions about the sick woman. Her husband, George Lynn, was evasive and probably ignorant. He admitted that Harriet had been to the dispensary and small infirmary that Southport called a hospital.

It was the only place in the entire Southern hemisphere where an operation could be performed legally. Most cases had to go to Northport, but Chris had been trying to expand. Apparently, she was determined to make Southport into another major center before she was called back to Earth.

Doc wondered why the villagers went there. They had no medical insurance with the Lobby; they couldn't afford it. Most villagers didn't have the cash, either. They were forced to mortgage their future work and that of their families to the drug plants that were run by the Lobby.

"And they just turned your wife away?" Doc asked. He couldn't quite believe that of Chris.

"Well, I dunno. She wouldn't talk much. Twice she went and they gave her something. Cost every cent I could borrow. Then this last time, they kept her a couple days before they let me come and get her. But now she's a lot worse."

Jake spun about, suddenly tense. "How'd you pay them last time, George?"

"Why, they didn't ask. I told her she could put up six months from me and the kids, but nobody said nothing about it. Just gave her back to me." He frowned slowly, his dull voice uncertain. "They told me they'd done all they could, not to bring her back. That's why she was so strong on getting Doc."

"I don't like it," Jake said flatly. "It stinks. They always charge. George, did they suggest she get in touch with Doc here?"

"Maybe they did, maybe not. Harriet did all the talking with them. I just do what she tells me, and she said to get Doc."

Jake swore. "It smells like a trap. Are you sure she's sick, George?"

"I felt her head and she sure had a fever." George Lynn was torn between his loyalties. "You know me, Doc. You fixed me up that time I had the red pip. I wouldn't pull nothing on you."

Doc had a feeling that Jake was probably right, but he vetoed the suggestion that they stop to look for spies. He had no time for that. If the woman was really sick, he had to get to her at once, and even that might be too late.

He remembered the woman, sickly from other treatment. He'd been forced to remove her inflamed tonsils a few months before. She'd whined and complained because he couldn't spend all his time attending her. She was a nag, a shrew, and a totally selfish woman. But that was her husband's worry, not his.

He dashed into the little house when they reached Einstein, and his first glance confirmed what George Lynn had said. The woman was sick, all right. She was running a high fever. Much too high.

She began whining and protesting at his having taken so long, but the pain soon forced her to stop.

"There may still be a chance," Doc told her husband brusquely. He threw the cleanest sheet onto a table and shoved it under the single light. "Keep out of the way—in the other room, if you can all pile in there. This isn't exactly aseptic, anyhow. You can boil a lot of water, if you want to help."

It would give them something to do and he could use the water to clean up. There was no time to wait for it, however. He had to sterilize with alcohol and carbolic acid, and hope. He bent over the woman, ripping her thin gown across to make room for the operation.

Then he swore.

Across her abdomen was the unhealed wound of a previous operation. They'd worked on her at Southport. They must have removed the appendix and then been shocked by the signs of infection. They weren't supposed to release a sick patient, but there was an easy out for them; they could remove her from the danger of spreading an unknown infection. Some doctors must have doped her up on sedatives and painkillers and sent her home, knowing that she would call him. For that matter, they might have noticed her unrecorded tonsillectomy and considered her fair bait.

He grabbed the ether and slapped a cone over her nose. She tried to protest; she never cooperated in anything. But the fumes of the ether he dipped onto the packing of the cone soon overcame that.

It was peritonitis, of course. The only thing to do was to go in and scrape and clean as best he could. It was a rotten job to have to do, and he should have had help. But he gritted his teeth and began. He couldn't trust anyone else to hold the instruments, even.

He cleaned the infection as best he could, knowing there was almost no chance. He used all the penicillin he dared. Then he began sewing up the incision. It was all he could do, except for dressing the wound with a sterile bandage. He reached for one, and stopped.

While he'd been working, the woman had died, far more quietly than she had ever lived.

It was probably the only gracious act of her life. But it was damning to Doc. They couldn't hide her death, and any investigation would show that someone had worked on her. To the Lobby, he would be the one who had murdered her.

Jake was waiting in the tractor. He took one look at Doc's face and made no inquiries.

They were more than a mile away when Jake pointed back. Small in the distance, but distinct against the sands, a gray Medical Corps tractor was coming. Either they'd had a spy in the village or they'd guessed the rate of her infection very closely. They must have hoped to catch Doc in the act, and they'd barely missed.

It wouldn't matter. Their pictures and what testimony they could force from the village should be enough to hang Doc.

CHAPTER SIX
Research

There had been a council the night following the death of Harriet Lynn. Somehow the word had spread through the villages and the chiefs had assembled in Jake's village. But they had brought no solution, and in the long run had been forced to accept Doc's decision.

"I'm not going to retire and hide," he'd told them, surprised at his own decision, but grimly determined. "You need me and I need you. I'll move every day in hopes the Lobby police won't find me, but I won't quit."

Now he was packing the things he most needed and getting ready to move. The small bottles in which he was trying to grow his cultures would need warmth. He shoved them into an inner pocket, and began surveying what must be left.

He was heading for his tractor when another battered machine drove up. It had a girl of about fourteen, with tears streaming down her face. She held out a pleading hand, and her voice was scared. "It's—it's mama!"

"Where?"

"Leibnitz."

Leibnitz was near enough. Doc started his tractor, motioning for the girl to lead the way. The little dwelling she led him to was at the edge of the village, looking more poverty-stricken than most.

Chris Ryan, and three of the Medical Lobby police were inside, waiting. The girl's mother was tied to the bed, with a collection of medical instruments laid out, but apparently the threat had been enough. No actual injury had been inflicted. Probably none had been intended seriously.

"I knew you'd answer that kind of call," Chris said coldly.

He grinned sickly. They'd wasted no time. "I hear it's more than you'll do, Chris. Congratulations! My patient died. You're lucky."

"She was certainly dead when my men took her picture. The print shows the death grimace clearly."

"Pretty. Frame it and keep it to comfort you when you feel lonely," he snapped.

She struck him across the mouth with the handle of her gun. Then she twisted out through the door quickly, heading for the tractor that had been camouflaged to look like those used by the villagers. The three police led him behind her.

A shout went up, and people began to rush onto the village street. But they were too late. By the time they reached Southport, Doc could see a trail of battered tractors behind, but there was nothing more the people could do. Chris had her evidence and her prisoner.

Judge Ben Wilson might have been Jake's brother. He was older and grayer, but the same expression lay on his face. He must have been the family black sheep, since his father had been president of Space Lobby. Instead of inheriting the position, Wilson had remained on Mars, safely out of the family's way.

He dropped the paper he was reading to frown at Chris. "This the fellow?"

She began formal charges, but he cut them off. "Your lawyer already had all that drawn up. I've been expecting you, Doctor. Doctor! Hnnf! You'd do a lot better home somewhere raising a flock of babies. Well, young fellow—so you're Feldman. Okay, your trial comes up day after tomorrow. Be a shame to lock you in Southport jail, a man of your importance. We'll just keep you here in the pending-trial room. It's a lot more comfortable."

Chris had been boiling slowly, and now she seemed to blow her safety valve. "Judge Wilson, your methods are your own business in local affairs. But this involves Earth Medical Lobby. I demand—"

"Tch, *tch*!" The judge stared at her reprovingly. "Young woman, you don't demand anything. This is Mars. If Space Lobby can stand me, I guess our friends over at Medical will have to. Or should I hold trial right now and find Feldman innocent for lack of evidence?"

"You wouldn't!" Chris cried. Then her face sobered suddenly. "I apologize. Medical is pleased to leave things in your hands, of course."

Wilson smiled. "Court's closed for today. Doc, I'll show you your cell. It's right next to my study, so I'm heading there anyhow."

He began shucking his robe while Chris went out with the police, her voice sharp and continual.

The cell was both reasonably escape-proof and comfortable, Doc saw, and he tried to thank the judge.

But the old man waved it aside. "Forget it. I just like to see that little termagant taken down. But don't count on my being soft. My methods may be a bit unusual—I always did like the courtroom scenes in the old books by that fellow Smith—but Space Lobby never had any reason to reverse my decisions. Anything you need?"

"Sure," Doc told him, grinning in spite of his bitterness. "A good biology lab and an electron microscope."

"Umm. How about a good optical mike and some stains? Just got them in on the last shipment. Figure they were meant for you anyhow, since Jake Mullens asked me to order them."

He went out and came back with the box almost at once. He snorted at Doc's incredulous thanks and moved off, his bedroom slippers slapping against the hard floor.

Doc stared after him. If he were a friend of Jake, willing to invent some excuse to get a microscope here...but it didn't matter. Friend or foe, his death sentence would be equally fatal. And there were other things to be thought of now. The little microscope was an excellent one, though only a monocular.

Doc's hands trembled as he drew his cultures out and began making up a slide. The sun offered the best source of light near the window, and he adjusted the instrument. Something began to come into view, but too faintly to be really visible.

He remembered the stains, trying to recall his biology courses. More by luck than skill, his fourth try gave him results.

Under two thousand powers, he could just see details. There were dozens of cells in his impure culture, but only one seemed unfamiliar. It was a long, worm-like thing, sharpened at both ends, with the three separate nuclei that were typical of Martian life forms. Nearby were a host of little rodlike squiggles just too small to see clearly.

Martian life! No Martian bug had ever proved harmful to men. Yet this was no mutated cell or virus from Earth; it was a new disease, completely different from all others. It was one where all Earth's centuries of experience with bacteria would be valueless—the first Martian disease. Unless this was simply some accidental contamination of his culture, not common to the other samples. He worked on until the light was too faint before putting the microscope aside.

By the time the trial commenced, however, he was sure of the cause of the disease. It *was* Martian. Crude as his cultures were, they had proved that.

The little courtroom was filled, mostly from the villages. Lou was there, along with others he had come to know. Then the sight of Jake caught Doc's eyes. The darned fool had no business there; he could get too closely mixed into the whole mess.

"Court's in session," Wilson announced. "Doc, you represented by counsel?"

Jake's voice answered. "Your Honor, I represent the defendant. I think you'll find my credentials in order."

Chris started to protest, but Wilson grinned. "Never lost your standing in spite of that little fracas thirty years ago, so far as I know. But the police thought you were a witness when you came walking in. Figured you were giving up."

"I never said so," Jake answered.

Chris was squirming angrily, but the florid man acting as counsel for Medical Lobby shook his head, bending over to whisper in her ear. He straightened. "No objection to counsel for the defense. We recognize his credentials."

"You're a fool, Matthews," the judge told him. "Jake was smarter than half the rest of Legal Lobby before he went native. Still can tie your tail to a can. Okay, let's start things. I'm too old to dawdle."

Doc lost track of most of what happened. This was totally unlike anything on Earth, though it might have been in keeping with the general casualness of the villages. Maybe the ritualistic routine of the Lobbies was driving those who could resist to the opposite extreme.

Chris was the final witness. Matthews drew comment of Feldman's former crime from her, and Jake made no protest, though Wilson seemed to expect one. Then she began sewing his shroud. There wasn't a fact that managed to emerge without slanting, though technically correct. Jake sat quietly, smiling faintly, and making no protests.

He got up lazily to cross-examine Chris. "Dr. Ryan, when Daniel Feldman was examined by the Captain of the *Navaho* after arriving at Mars station, did you identify him then as having been Dr. Daniel Feldman?"

She glanced at Matthews, who seemed puzzled but unconcerned. "That's correct," she admitted. "But—"

"And you later saw him delivered to the surface of Mars. Is that also correct?" When she assented, Jake hesitated. Then he frowned. "What did you do then? Did you report him or send anyone to look after him or anything like that?"

"Certainly not," she answered. "He was no—"

"You did absolutely nothing about him after you identified him and saw him delivered here? You're quite sure of that?"

"I did nothing."

Jake stood quietly for a moment, then shrugged. "No more questions."

Matthews finished things in a plea for the salvation of all humanity from the danger of such men as Daniel Feldman. He was looking smug, as was Chris.

Wilson turned to Jake. "Has the defense anything to say?"

"A few things, Your Honor." Jake stood up, suddenly looking certain and pleased. "We are happy to admit everything factual the Lobby had testified. Daniel Feldman performed a surgical operation on Harriet Lynn in the village of Einstein. But when has it been illegal for a member of the Medical profession to perform an operation, even with small chance of success, within an accepted area for such operation? There has been no evidence adduced that any crime or act of even unethical conduct was committed."

That brought Chris and Matthews to their feet. Wilson was relaxed again, looking as if he'd swallowed a whole cage of canaries. He banged his gavel down.

Jake picked up two ragged and dog-eared volumes from his table. "Case of Harding vs. Southport, 2043, establishes that a Lobby is responsible for any member on Mars. It is also responsible for informing the authorities of any criminal conduct on the part of its members or any former member known to it. Failure to report shall be considered an admission that the Lobby recognizes the member as one in good standing and accepts responsibility for that member's conduct.

"At the time Daniel Feldman arrived, Dr. Christina Ryan was the highest appointed representative of Medical Lobby in Southport, with full authority. She identified Feldman as having been a doctor, without stipulating any change in status. She made no further report to any authority concerning Daniel Feldman's presence here. It seems obvious that Medical Lobby at Southport thereby accepted Daniel Feldman as a doctor in good standing for whose conduct the Lobby accepted full responsibility."

Wilson studied the book Jake held out, and nodded. "Seems pretty clear-cut to me," he agreed, passing the book on to Matthews. "There's still the charge that Dr. Feldman operated outside a hospital."

"No reason he shouldn't," Jake said. He handed over the other volume. "This is the charter for Medical Lobby on Mars. Medical Lobby agrees to perform all necessary surgical and medical services for the planet, though at the signing of this charter there was no hospital on Mars. Necessarily, Medical Lobby agreed to perform surgery outside of any hospital, then. But to make it plainer, there's a later paragraph—page 181—that defines each hospital zone as extending not less than three nor more than one hundred miles. Einstein is about one hundred and ten miles from the nearest hospital at Southport, so Einstein comes under the original charter provisions. Dr. Feldman was forced by charter provisions to protect the good name of his Lobby by undertaking any necessary surgery in Einstein."

He waited until Matthews had scanned that book, then took it back and began packing a big bag. Doc saw that his possessions and the microscope were already in the bag. The old man paid no attention to the arguments of Matthews before the bench.

Abruptly Wilson pounded his gavel. "This court finds that Dr. Daniel Feldman is qualified to practice all the arts and skills of the medical profession on Mars and that he acted ethically in the performance of his duties in the case of the deceased Harriet Lynn," he ruled. "The costs of the case shall be billed to Medical Lobby of Southport."

He took off his robe and moved rapidly toward his private quarters. Court was closed.

Doc got up shakily, not daring to believe fully what he had heard. He started toward Jake, trying to avoid bumping into Chris. But she would not be avoided. She stood in front of him, screaming accusations and threats that reminded him of the only fight they'd ever had during their brief marriage.

When she ran down, he finally met her eyes. "You're a helluva doctor," he told her harshly. "You spend all your time fighting me when there's a plague out there that may be worse than any disease we've ever known. Take a look at what lies under the black specks on your corpses. You'll find the first Martian disease. And maybe if you begin working on that now, you can learn to be a real doctor in time to do something about it. But I doubt it."

She fell back from him then. "Research! You've been doing unauthorized research!"

"Prove it," he suggested. "But you'd be a lot smarter to try some yourself, and to hell with your precious rules."

He followed Jake out to the tractor.

Surprisingly, the old man was sweating now. He shook his head at Doc's look, and his grin was uncertain.

"Matthews is an incompetent," he said. "They could have had you, Doc. That charter is so sloppy a man can prove anything by it, and building a hospital here did bring in Earth rules. Wilson went out on a limb in letting you go. But I guess we got away with it. Let's get out of here."

Doc climbed into the tractor more soberly. They had escaped this time. But there would be another time, and he was pretty sure that would be Chris' round. He had no intention of giving up his research.

CHAPTER SEVEN
Plague

Dr. Feldman leaned back from his microscope and lighted another bracky weed. He glanced about the room and sighed wearily. Maybe he'd been better off when he had no friends and couldn't risk the safety of others in an effort to do research that was the highest crime on two worlds.

The evidence of his work was hidden thirty feet beyond his former laboratory in Jake's village, with a tunnel that led from another root-cellar. The theory was the old one that the best place to avoid discovery was where you had already been discovered. If their spies had identified his former hangout, they'd never expect to have him set up research nearby. It was a nice theory, but he wasn't sure of it.

Jake looked up from a cot where he'd been watching the improvised culture incubator. "Stop tearing yourself to bits, Doc. We know the danger and we're still darned glad to have you here working on this."

"I'm trying to put myself together into a whole man," Doc told him. "But I seem to come out wholly a fool."

"Yeah, sure. Sometimes it takes a fool to get things done; wise men wait too long for the right time. How's the bug hunt?"

Doc grunted in disgust and swung back to the microscope. Then he gave up as his tired eyes refused to focus. "Why don't you people revolt?"

"They tried it twice. But they were just a bunch of pariahs shipped here to live in peonage. They couldn't do much. The first time Earth cut off shipments and starved them. Next time the villages had the answer to that but the cities had to fight for Earth or starve, so they whipped us. And there's always the threat that Earth could send over unmanned war rockets loaded with fissionables."

"So it's hopeless?"

"So nothing! The Lobbies are poisoning themselves, like cutting off Medical service until they cut themselves out of a job. It's just a matter of time. Go back to the bugs, Doc."

Doc sighed and reached for his notes. "I wish I knew more Martian history. I've been wondering whether this bug may not have been what killed off the old Martians. Something had to do it, the way they disappeared. I wish I knew enough to make an investigation of those ruins out there."

"Durwood!" Jake had propped himself on an elbow, staring at Doc in surprise.

Doc scowled. "Clive Durwood, you mean? The archeologist who dug up what little we know about the ruins?"

"Yeah, before he went back to Earth and started living off his lectures. He came here again three years ago and dropped dead in Edison on the way to some other ruins. Heart failure, they called it, though it was more like the two old farmers who ran themselves to death last month. I saw him when they buried him. His face looked funny, and I think he had those little specks, though I may remember wrong." He grimaced. "Mars is tough, Doc; it has to be. Some of the plant seeds Durwood found in the ruins grew! Maybe your bugs waited a million years till we came along."

"What about the farmers? Did they meet Durwood?"

Jake nodded. "Must have. He lived in their village most of the time."

Doc went through his notes. He'd asked for reports on all deaths, and he finally found the account. The two old men had been nervous and fidgety for weeks. They were twins, living by themselves, and nobody paid much attention. Then one morning both were seen running wildly in circles. The village managed to tie them up, but they died of exhaustion shortly after.

It wasn't a pretty picture. The disease might have an incubation period of nearly fifteen years, judging by the length of time it had taken to hit Durwood. It must spread from person to person during an early contagious stage, leaving widening circles behind Durwood and those first infected. When matured, any other sickness would set it off, with few symptoms of its own. But without help, it still killed its victims, apparently driving them madly toward frenzied physical effort.

He studied the culture on a slide again. He'd tried Koch's method to get a pure strain, splattering the bugs onto a native starchy root and plucking off individual colonies. About twenty specimens had been treated with every chemical he could find. So far he'd found a few things that seemed to stop their growth, but nothing that killed them, except stuff far too harsh to use in living tissue.

He had nearly forty cases of deaths that showed symptoms now, and he went back over them, looking for anything in common that went back ten to twenty years before death. There were no rashes nor blisters. A few had had apparent colds, but such were too common to mean anything.

Only one thing appeared, about fourteen years before their deaths. The people interviewed about the victims might be vague about most things, but they remembered the time when "Jim had the jumping headache."

"Jake," Doc called, "what's jumping headache? Most people seem to have it some time or other, but I haven't run across a case of it."

"Sure you have, Doc. Mamie Brander's little girl a few weeks ago. Feels like your pulse is going to rip your skull off, right here. Can't eat because chewing drives you crazy. Back of your head, neck and shoulders swell up for about a week. Then it goes away."

Then it goes away—for fourteen years, until it comes back to kill!

Doc stared at his charts in sudden horror. It was a new disease—thought to be some virus, but not considered dangerous. Selznik's migraine, according to medical usage; you treated it with hot pads and anodyne, and it went away easily enough.

He'd seen hundreds of such cases on Earth. There must be millions who had been hit by it. The patent-medicine branch of the Lobby had even brought out something called Nograine to use for self-treatment.

"Something important?" Jake wanted to know.

Feldman nodded. "How much weight do you swing in other villages, Jake?"

"People sort of do me favors when I ask," Jake admitted. "Like swiping those medical journals from Northport for you, or like Molly Badger getting that job as maid to spy on Chris Ryan. Name it and I'll do my best."

Doc had a vague idea of village politics, but he had more important things to think of. Most of his foul mood had disappeared with the clue he'd stumbled on, and his chief worry now was to clinch the facts.

Feldman considered the problem. "I want a report on every case of jumping headache in every village—who had it, when, and how old they were. This place first, but every village you can reach. And I'll want someone to take a letter to Chris Ryan."

Jake frowned at that, but went out to issue instructions. Doc sat down at a battered old typewriter. Writing Chris might do no good, but some warning had to be gotten through to Earth, where the vast resources of Medical Lobby could be thrown into the task of finding the cause and cure of the disease. The connection with Selznik's migraine had to be reported. If something could blast the Lobby into action, it wouldn't matter quite so much what they did to him. He wasn't foolish enough to expect gratitude from them, but he was getting used to the idea that his days were numbered. The plague was more important than what happened to him.

The letter had been dispatched by the time Jake returned. "Here's the dope for this village. Everybody accounted for except you."

"Never had it, Jake." Feldman went down the list. "Most of it fourteen years ago. That fits. About the only exceptions are the kids who seem to get it between the ages of two and three. Eighty-seven out of ninety-one!"

He stared at the figures sickly. Most of the village not only had the plague but must be near the end of the incubation period. It looked as if most of the village would be dead before another year passed.

"Bad?" Jake asked.

"The first symptom of Martian fever."

The old man whistled, the lines around his eyes tightening. "Must be me," he decided. "I'm the guy who must have brought it here, then. I used to spend a lot of time with Durwood at his diggings!"

There was a constant commotion all that day and the next as runners went out to the villages and returned with reports. The variation from village to village was only slight. Most of Mars seemed to have advanced cases of Martian fever.

Without animals for investigation and study, real research was difficult. Doc also needed an electron microscope. He was fairly sure that the disease must travel through the nerves, but he had found no proof beyond the hard lump at the base of the neck. There it was a fair-sized organism. Elsewhere he could find nothing, until the black specks developed.

His eyes ached from trying to see more than was visible in the microscope. The tantalizing suggestions of filaments around the nuclei might be the form of plague that was contagious. They might even be the true form of the bug, with the bigger cell only a transition stage. There were a number of diseases that involved complicated changes in the organisms that caused them. But he couldn't be sure.

He finally buried his head in his hands, trying to do by pure thought what he couldn't do in any other way. And even there, he lacked training. He was a doctor, not a xenobiologist. Research training had been taboo in school, except for a favored few.

The reports continued to come in, confirming the danger. They seemed to have the worst plague on their hands in all human history; and nobody who could do anything about it even knew of it.

"Molly reports that your letter got some results," Jake reported. "Chris Ryan brought home one of the electron microscopes and a bunch of equipment from the hospital pathology room. Think she'll get anywhere?"

Doc doubted it. Damn it, he hadn't meant for her to try it, though she might have authority for routine experiments. But it was like her to refuse to pass on the word without trying to prove her own suspicion of him first.

He tried to comfort himself with the fact that some men were immune, or seemed so; about three out of a hundred showed no signs. If that immunity was hereditary, it might save the race. If not...

Jake came in at twilight with a grim face. "More news from Molly. The Lobby is starting out to comb every village with a fault-finder, starting here. And this hole will show up like a sore thumb. Better start packing. We gotta be out of here in less than an hour!"

CHAPTER EIGHT
Fool

Three days later, Doc saw his first runner.

The tractor was churning through the sand just before sundown, heading toward another one-night stand at a new village. Lou was driving, while Doc and Jake brooded silently in the back, paying no attention to the colors that were blazoned over the dunes. The cat-and-mouse game was getting to Doc. There was no real assurance that the village they were approaching might not be the target the Lobby had chosen for the next investigation.

Lou braked the tractor to a sudden halt, and pointed.

A figure was running frantically over one of the low dunes with the little red sun behind him. He seemed headed toward them, but as he drew nearer they could see that he had no definite direction. He simply ran, pumping his legs frantically as if all the devils of hell were after him. His body swayed from side to side in exhaustion, but his arms and legs pumped on.

"Stop him!" Jake ordered, and Lou swung the tractor. It halted squarely in the runner's path, and the figure struck against it and toppled.

The legs went on pumping, digging into the dirt and gravel, but the man was too far gone to rise. Jake and Lou shoved him through the doors into the tractor and Doc yanked off his aspirator.

The man was giving vent to a kind of ululating cry, weakened now almost to a whine that rose and fell with the motion of his legs. Sweat had once streaked his haggard face, but it was dry and blanched to a pasty gray.

Doc injected enough narcotic to quiet a maddened bull. It had no effect, except to upset the rhythm of the arms and legs. It took five more minutes for the man to die.

The specks were larger this time—the size of periods in twelve-point type. The lump at the base of the skull was as big as a small hen's egg.

"From Edison, like the others so far. Jack Kooley," Jake answered Doc's question. "Durwood spent a lot of time here on his first expedition, so it's getting the worst of it."

Doc pulled the aspirator mask back over the man's face and they carried him out and laid him on a low dune. They couldn't risk returning the corpse to its people.

This was only the primary circle of infection, direct from Durwood. The second circle could be ten times as large, as the infection spread from one to a few to many. So far it was localized. But it wouldn't stay that way.

Doc climbed slowly out of the tractor, lugging his small supplies of equipment, while Jake made arrangements for them to spend the night in a deserted house. But the figure of the runner and his own failures to find more about the disease kept haunting Doc. He began setting up his equipment grimly.

"Better get some sleep," Jake suggested. "You're a mite more tired than you think. Anyhow, I thought you told me you couldn't do any more with what you've got."

Feldman looked at the supplies he had spread out, and shook his head wearily. He'd been over every chemical and combination a dozen times, without results that showed in the limited magnification of the optical mike.

He snapped the case shut and hit the rude table with the heel of his hand. "There are other supplies. Jake, do you have any signal to get in touch with Molly at the Ryan house?"

"Three raps on the rear left window. I'll get Lou."

"No!" Doc came to his feet, reaching for his jacket. "They're looking for three men now. It's safer if I go alone—and I'm the only one who knows what supplies are needed. With luck, I may even get the electron mike. Got a gun I can borrow?"

Jake found one somewhere, an old revolver with a few loads. He began protesting, but Doc overruled him sharply. Three men could no more fight off the police than one, if they were spotted. He swung toward the tractor.

"You'd better start spreading the word on everything we know. If people realize they're already safe or doomed it'll be better than having them going crazy to avoid contagion."

"Most of the villages know already," Jake told him. "And damn it, get back here, Doc. If you can't make it, turn tail quick, and we'll think of something else."

Southport seemed normal enough as Doc drove through its streets. The stereo house was open, and the little shops were brightly lighted. He stopped once to pull a copy of Southport's little newspaper from a dispenser. All was quiet on its front page, too.

As usual, though, the facts were buried inside. The editorial was pouring too much oil on the waters in its lauding of the role of Medical Lobby on Mars for no apparent reason. The death notices no longer listed the cause of death. Medical knew something was up, at least, and was worried.

He parked the tractor behind Chris' house and slipped to the proper window. Everything was seemingly quiet there. At his knock, the shade was drawn back, and he caught a brief glimpse of Molly looking out. A moment later she opened the rear lock to let him into the kitchen.

"Shh. She's still up, I think. What can I do, Doc?"

He tried to smile at her. "Hide me until it's safe to get into her laboratory. I've got to—"

The inner kitchen was kicked open and Chris stood beyond it, holding a cocked gun in her hand.

"It took longer than I expected, Dan," she said quietly. "But after your letter, I knew you'd swallow the bait. You bloody fool! Did you really believe I'd start doing research here just because of your imaginings?"

He slumped slowly back against the sink. "So this is a fool's errand, then? There never was any equipment here?"

"The equipment's here—in my office. I guessed your spies would report it, so it had to be here. But it won't help you now, pariah Feldman!"

He came from his braced position against the sink like a spring uncoiling. He expected her to shoot, but hoped the surprise would ruin her aim. Then it was too late, and his boot hit the gun savagely, knocking it from her hand. Life in the villages had hardened him surprisingly. She was comparatively helpless in his hands. A few minutes later, he had her bound securely with surgical tape Molly brought him. She raged furiously in the chair where he'd dumped her, then gave up.

"They'll get you, Daniel Feldman!" Surprisingly, there was no rage in her voice now. "You won't get away from us. The planet isn't big enough."

"I got away from your trial," he reminded her. "And I got away and lived when you left me without a chance on the ground of the spaceport."

She laughed harshly. "*You* got away then? You fool, who do you think gave you the extra battery so you could live long enough to be helped at the spaceport? Who hired a fool like Matthews so you wouldn't get the death sentence you deserved? Who let you get away as an herb doctor for months before you set yourself up as God and a traitor to mankind again?"

It shook him, as it was probably intended to do. How had she known about the extra battery? He'd always assumed that Ben had returned to give it to him. But in that case, Chris couldn't know of it. Then he hardened himself again. In the old days, she'd always had one trump card he couldn't beat and hadn't expected. But too much was involved for games now.

"Any police around, Molly?" he asked.

Molly came back a minute later to report that everything looked clear and to show him where the equipment had been set up in Chris' office. It was all there, including the electron mike—a beautiful little portable model. There was even a small incubator with its own heat source into which he immediately transferred the little bottles he'd been keeping warm against his skin. Most of the equipment had never been unpacked, which made loading it onto his tractor ridiculously easy.

"Better come with me now, Molly," he suggested at last. Then he turned to Chris, who was watching him with almost no expression. "You can wriggle your chair to the phone in half an hour, I guess. Knock the phone off and yell for help. It's better than you deserve, unless you really did leave me that battery."

"You won't get away with it," she told him again, calmly this time.

"No," he admitted. "Probably not. But maybe the human race will, if I have time to find an answer to the plague you won't see under your nose. But you won't get away with it, either. In the long run, your kind never do."

Molly was sniffling as they drove away. It had probably been the best life she'd known, Doc supposed. Chris could be kind to menials. But now Molly's work was done, and she'd have to disappear into the villages. He let her off at the first village and drove on alone. He was itching to get to the microscope now, hardly able to wait through the long journey back to Jake. His impatience grew with each mile.

Finally he gave up. He swung the tractor into a small gulley between sand dunes, left the motor idling and pulled down the shades the villagers used for blackout traveling. There was power enough for the mike here, and the cab was big enough for what he had to do.

He mounted the mike on the tractor seat and began laying out the collection of smears and cultures he had brought. It had been years since he'd made a film for the electron mike, but he found it all came back to him as he worked.

His hands were sweating with tension as he inserted the first film into the chamber. He had the magnetic "lenses" set for twenty thousand power, but a quick glance showed it was too weak. He raised the power to fifty thousand.

The filaments were there, clear and distinct.

He turned on the little tape recorder that had been part of Chris' equipment and set the microphone where he could dictate into it without stopping to make clumsy notes. He readjusted the focus carefully, carrying on a running commentary.

Then he gasped. Each of the little filaments carried three tiny darker sections; each was a cell, complete in itself, with the typical Martian triple nucleus.

He put a film with a tiny section of the nerve tissue from a corpse into the chamber next, and again a quick glance at the screen was enough. The filaments were there, thickly crowded among nerve cells. They *did* travel along the nerves to reach the base of the brain before the larger lump could form.

A specimen from one of the black specks was even more interesting. The filaments were there, but some were changed or changing into tiny, round cells, also with the triple dark spots of nuclei. Those must be the final form that was released to infect others. Probably at first these multiplied directly in epithelial tissue, so that there was a rapid contagion of infection. Eventually, they must form the filaments that invaded the nerves and caused the brief bodily reaction that was Selznik's migraine. Then the body adapted to them and they began to incubate slowly, developing into the large cells he had first seen. When "ripe", the big cells broke apart into millions of the tiny round ones that went back to the nerve endings, causing the black spots and killing the host.

He knew his enemy now, at least.

He reached for the controls, increasing the magnification. He would lose resolution, but he might find something more at the extreme limits of the mike.

Something wet and cold gushed into his face. He jerked back, trying to wipe it off, but it was already evaporating, and there was a thick, acrid odor in the cab. He grabbed for his aspirator, then tried to reach the airlock. But paralysis was already spreading through him, and he toppled to the floor before he could escape.

When he came to, it was morning outside, and Chris was waiting inside the cab with two big Lobby policemen. A hypo in her hand must have been what revived him.

She touched the electron microscope with something like affection. "The Lobby technicians did a good job on this, don't you think, Dan? I warned you, but you wouldn't listen. And now we've even got your own taped words to prove you were doing forbidden research. Fool!"

She shook her head pityingly as the tractor began moving with two others toward Southport.

"You and your phony diseases. A little skin disorder, Selznik's migraine, and a few cases of psychosis to make a new disease. Do you think Medical Lobby can't check on such simple things? Or didn't you expect us to hear of your open talk of revolt and realize you were planning to create some new germ to wipe out the Earth forces. Maybe those runners of yours were real, mass murderer!"

She drew out another hypo and shoved the needle into his arm. Necrosynth—enough to keep him unconscious for twenty-four hours. He started to curse her, but the drug acted before he could complete the thought.

CHAPTER NINE
Judgement

Doc woke to see sunlight shining through a heavily barred window that must be in the official Southport jail. He waited a few minutes for his head to clear and then sat up; necrosynth left no hangover, at least.

The sound of steps outside was followed by the squeak of a key in the lock. "Fifteen minutes, Judge Wilson," a voice said.

"Thank you, officer." Wilson came into the cell, carrying a tray of breakfast and a copy of the Northport *Gazette*. He began unloading bracky weeds from his pocket while Doc attacked the breakfast.

"They tossed the book at you, Doc," he said. "You haven't got a chance, and there's nothing the villages can do. Trial's set for tomorrow at Northport, and it's in closed session. We can't get you off this time."

Doc nodded. "Thanks for coming, even if there's nothing you can do. I've been living on borrowed time for a year, anyhow, so I have no right to kick. But who's 'we'?"

"The villages. I've been part of their organization for years." The old man sighed heavily. "You might say a revolution has been going on since I can remember, though most villagers don't know it. We've just been waiting our time. Now we've stopped waiting and the rifles will be coming out—rifles made in village shops. The villages are going to rebel, even if we're all dead of plague in a month."

Doc Feldman nodded and reached for the bracky. He knew that this was their way of trying to make him feel his work hadn't been for nothing, and he was grateful for

Wilson's visit. "It was a good year for me. Damned good. But time's running short. I'd better brief you on the latest on the plague."

Wilson began making notes until Doc was finished. Finally he got up as steps sounded from the hall. "Anything else?"

"Just a guess. A lot of Earth germs can't live in Mars-normal flesh; maybe this can't live in Earth-normal. Tell them so long for me."

"So long, Doc." He shook hands briefly and was waiting at the door when the guard opened it.

An hour later, the Lobby police took Feldman to the Northport shuttle rocket. They had some trouble on the way; a runner cut down the street, with the crowds frantically rushing out of his way. Terror was reaching the cities already.

Doc flashed a look at Chris. "Mob hysteria. Like flying saucers and wriggly tops, I suppose?" he asked, before the guard could stop him.

They locked his legs, but left his hands free in the rocket. He unfolded the paper Wilson had brought and buried his face in it. Then he swore. They *were* explaining the runners as a case of mob hysteria!

Northport was calmer. Apparently they had yet to have first-hand experience with the plague. But now nothing seemed quite real to Doc, even when they locked him into the big Northport jail. The whole ritual of the Lobbies seemed like a fantasy after the villages.

It snapped back into focus, however, when they led him into the trial room of the Medical Lobby building. It was a smaller version of his trial on Earth. Fear washed in by association. The complete lack of humanity in the procedure was something from a half-remembered and horrible past.

The presiding officer asked the routine question: "Is the prisoner represented by counsel?"

Blane, the dapper little prosecutor, arose quickly. "The prisoner is a pariah, Sir Magistrate."

"Very well. The court will accept the protective function for the prisoner. You may proceed."

I'll be judge, I'll be jury. And prosecution and defense. It made for a lot less trouble. Of course, if Space Lobby had asserted interest, it would have gone to a supposedly neutral court. But as usual, Space was happy to leave it in the hands of Medical.

The tape was played as evidence. Doc frowned. The words were his, but there had been a lot of editing that subtly changed the import of his notes.

"I protest," he challenged. "It's not an accurate version."

The Lobby magistrate turned a wooden face to him. "Does the prisoner have a different version to introduce?"

"No, but—"

"The evidence is accepted. One of the prisoner's six protests will be charged against him."

Blane smiled smoothly and held up a small package. "We wish to introduce this drug as evidence that the prisoner is a confirmed addict, morally irresponsible under addiction. This is a package of so-called bracky weed, a vile and noxious substance found in his possession."

"It has alkaloids no more harmful than nicotine," Feldman stated sharply.

"Do you contend that you find the taste pleasing?" Blane asked.

"It's bitter, but I've gotten used to it."

"I've tasted it," the magistrate said. "Evidence accepted. Two deductions, one for irregularity of presentation."

Doc shrugged and sat back. He'd tested his rights and found what he expected. It was hard to see now how he had ever accepted such procedure. Jake must be right; they'd been in power too long, and were making the mistake of taking the velvet glove off the iron fist and flailing about for the sheer pleasure of power.

It dragged on, while he became a greater and greater monster on the record. But finally it was over, and the magistrate turned to Feldman. "You may present your defense."

"I ask complete freedom of expression," Doc said formally.

The magistrate nodded. "This is a closed court. Permission granted. The recording will be scrambled."

The last bit ruined most of the purpose Doc had in mind. But it was too late to change. He could only hope that some one of the Medical men present would remember something of what he said.

"I have nothing to say for myself," he began. "It would be useless. But I had to do what I did. There's a plague outside. I've studied that plague, and I have knowledge which must be used against it…"

He sat down in three minutes. It had been useless.

Blane arose, with a smile still plastered on his face. "We, of course, recognize the existence of a new contagion, but I believe we have established that this is one disseminated by the prisoner himself, and probably not directly contagious. There have been many cases of fanatics ready to destroy humanity to eliminate those they hate. Now, surely, the prisoner has himself left no question of his attitude. He asserts he has knowledge and skill greater than the entire Medical Research staff. He has attempted to intimidate us by threats. He is clearly psychopathic, and dangerously so. The prosecution rests."

The guards took Doc into the anteroom, where he was supposed to hear nothing that went on. But their curiosity was stronger than their discretion, and the door remained a trifle ajar.

The magistrate began the discussion. "The case seems firm enough. It's fortunate Dr. Ryan acted so quickly, with some of the people getting nervous. Perhaps it might be wise to publicize our verdict."

"My thought exactly," Blane agreed. "If we show Feldman is responsible and that Medical is eliminating the source of the infection, it may have a stabilizing effect."

"Let's hope so. The sentence will have to be death, of course. We can't let such a rebellious psychopath live. But this needs something more, it seems. You've prepared a recommendation, I suppose."

"There was the case of Albrecht Delier," Blane suggested. "Something like that should have good publicity impact."

It struck Doc that they sounded as if they believed themselves—as the witch-burners had believed in witches. He was sweating when the guards led him before the bench.

The magistrate rolled a pen slowly across his fingers as his eyes raked Feldman. "Pariah Daniel Feldman, you have been found guilty on all counts. Furthermore, your guilt must be shared by that entire section of Mars known as the villages. Therefore the entire section shall be banned and forbidden any and all services of the Medical Lobby for a period of one year."

"Sir Magistrate!" One of the members of Southport Hospital staff was on his feet. "Sir Magistrate, we can't cut them off completely."

"We must, Dr. Harkness. I appreciate the fine humanitarian tradition of our Lobby which lies behind your protest, but at such a time as this the good of the body politic requires drastic measures. Why not see me after court, and we can discuss it then?"

He turned back to Feldman, and his face was severe.

"The same education which has produced such fine young men as Dr. Harkness was wasted on you and perverted to endanger the whole race. No punishment can equal your crimes, but there is one previously invoked for a particularly horrible case, and it seems fitting that you should be the fourth so sentenced.

"Daniel Feldman, you are sentenced to be taken in to space beyond planetary limits, together with all material used by you in the furtherance of your criminal acts. There you shall be placed into a spacesuit containing sufficient oxygen for one hour of life, and no more. You and your contaminated possessions shall then be released into space, to drift there through all eternity as a warning to other men.

"This sentence shall be executed at the earliest possible moment, and Dr. Christina Ryan is hereby commissioned to observe such execution. And may God have mercy on your soul!"

CHAPTER TEN
Execution

The hours of waiting were blurred for Doc. There were periods when fear clogged his throat and left him gasping with the need to scream and beat his cell walls. There were also times when it didn't seem to matter, and when his only thoughts were for the villages and the plague.

They brought him the papers, where he was painted as a monster beside whom Jack the Ripper and Albrecht Delier were gentle amateurs. They were trying to focus all fear and resentment on him. Maybe it was working. There were screaming crowds outside the jail, and the noise of their hatred was strong enough to carry through even the atmosphere of Mars. But there were also signs that the Lobby was worried, as if afraid that some attempt might still be made to rescue him.

He'd looked forward to the trip to the airport as a way of judging public reaction. But apparently the Lobby had no desire to test that. The guards led him up to the roof of the jail, where a rocket was waiting. The landing space was too small for one of the station shuttles, but a little Northport-Southport shuttle was parked there after what must have been a difficult set-down. The guards tested Doc's manacles and forced him into the shuttle.

Inside, Chris was waiting, carrying an official automatic. There was also a young pilot, looking nervous and unhappy. He was muttering under his breath as the guards locked Doc's legs to a seat and left.

"All right," Chris ordered. "Up ship!"

"I tell you we're overweight with you. I wasn't counting on three for the trip," the pilot protested. "The only thing that will get this into orbit with the station is faith. I'm loaded with every drop of fuel she'll hold and it still isn't enough."

"That's your problem," Chris told him firmly. "You've got your orders, and so have I. Up ship!"

If she had her own worries about the shuttle, she didn't show it. Chris had never been afraid to do what she felt she should. The pilot stared at her doubtfully and finally turned back to his controls, still muttering.

The shuttle lifted sluggishly, but there was no great difficulty. Doc could see that there was even some fuel remaining when they slipped into the tube at the orbital station. Chris went out, and other guards came in to free him.

"So long, Dr. Feldman," the pilot called softly as they led him out. Then the guards shoved him through the airlock into the station. Fifteen minutes later he was locked into one of the cabins of the *Iroquois*, with all his possessions stacked beside him.

He grinned wryly. As an honest worker on the *Navaho* he'd been treated like an animal. Now, as a human fiend, he was installed in a luxury cabin of the finest ship of the fleet, with constant spin to give a feeling of weight and more room than the entire tube crew had known.

He roamed the cabin until he found a little collapsible table. He set the electron microscope up on that and plugged it in. It seemed a shame that good equipment should be wasted along with his life. He wondered if they would really throw it out into space with him. Probably they would.

He pushed a button on the call board over the table and asked for the steward. There was a long wait, as if the procedure were being checked with some authority, but finally he received a surly acknowledgement. "Steward. Whatcha want?"

"How's the chance of getting some food?"

"You're on first-class."

They could afford it, Doc decided. He wouldn't cost them much, considering the distance he was going. "Bring me two complete dinners—one Earth-normal and one Mars-normal."

"Okay, Feldman. But if you think you can suicide that way, you're wrong. You may be sick, but you'll be alive when they dump you."

A sharp click interrupted him. "That's enough, Steward. Captain Everts speaking. Dr. Feldman, you have my apologies. Until you reach your destination, you are my passenger and entitled to every consideration of any other passenger except freedom of movement through the ship. I am always available for legitimate complaints."

Feldman shook his head. He'd heard of such men. But he'd thought the species extinct.

The steward brought his food in a thoroughly chastened manner. He managed to find space for it and came to attention. "Is that all—sir?"

For a moment, as the smell of real steak reached him, Doc regretted the fact that his metabolism had been switched. Then he shrugged. A little wouldn't hurt him, though there was no proper nourishment in it. He squeezed some of the gravy and bits of meat into one of his bottles, sticking to his purpose; then he fell to on the rest. But after a few bites, it was queerly unsatisfactory. The seemingly unappealing Mars-normal ragout suited his current tastes better, after all.

Once the steward had cleared away the dishes, Doc went to work. It was better than wasting his time in dread. He might even be able to leave some notes behind.

A gong sounded, and a red light warned him that acceleration was due. He finished with his bottles, put them into the incubator, and piled into his bunk, swallowing one of the tablets of morphetal the ship furnished.

Acceleration had ended, and a simple breakfast was waiting when he awoke. There was also a red flashing light over the call board. He flipped the switch while reaching for the coffee.

"Captain Everts," the speaker said. "May I join you in your cabin?"

"Come ahead," Feldman invited. He cut off the switch and glanced at the clock on the wall. There were less than eleven hours left to him.

Everts was a trim man of forty, erect but not rigid. There was neither friendliness nor hostility in his glance. His words were courteous as Doc motioned toward the tray of breakfast. "I've already eaten, thank you."

He accepted a chair. His voice was apologetic when he began. "This is a personal matter which I perhaps have no right to bring up. But my wife is greatly worried about this plague. I violate no confidence in telling you there is considerable unease, even on Earth, according to messages I have received. The ship physician believes Mrs. Everts may have the plague, but isn't sure of the symptoms. I understand you are quite expert."

Doc wondered about the physician. Apparently there was another man who placed his patients above anything else, though he was probably meticulous about obeying all actual rules. There was no law against listening to a pariah, at least.

"When did she have Selznik's migraine?" he asked.

"About thirteen years ago. We went through it together, shortly after having our metabolism switched during the food shortage of '88."

Doc felt carefully at the base of the Captain's skull; the swelling was there. He asked a few questions, but there could be no doubt.

"Both of you must have it, Captain, though it won't mature for another year. I'm sorry."

"There's no hope, then?"

Doc studied the man. But Everts wasn't the sort to dicker even for his life. "Nothing that I've found, Captain. I have a clue, but I'm still working on it. Perhaps if I could leave a few notes for your physician—"

It was Everts' turn to shake his head. "I'm sorry, Dr. Feldman. I have orders to burn out your cabin when you leave. But thank you." He got to his feet and left as quietly and erectly as he had entered.

Doc tore up his notes bitterly. He paced his cabin slowly, reading out the hours while his eyes lingered on the little bottle of cultures. At times the fear grew in him, but he mastered it. There was half an hour left when he began opening the little bottles and making his films.

He was still not finished when steps echoed down the hall, but he was reasonably sure of his results. The bug could not grow in Earth-normal tissue.

Three men entered the room. One, dressed in a spacesuit, held out another suit to him. The other two began gathering up everything in the cabin and stowing it neatly into a sack designed to protect freight for a limited time in a vacuum.

Doc forced his hands to steadiness with foolish pride and began climbing into the suit. He reached for the helmet, but the man shook his head, pointing to the oxygen gauge. There would be exactly one hour's supply of oxygen when he was thrown out and it still lacked five minutes of the deadline.

They marched him down the hallway, to meet Everts coming toward them. There were still three minutes left when they reached the airlock, with its inner door already open. The spacesuited man climbed into it and began strapping down so that the rush of air would not sweep him outward when the other seal was released.

Doc had saved one bracky weed. Now he raised it to his lips, fumbling for a light.

Everts stepped forward and flipped a lighter. Doc inhaled deeply. Fear was thick in every muscle, and he needed the smoke desperately. Then he caught himself.

"Better change your metabolism back to Earth-normal, Captain Everts," he said, and his voice was so normal that he hardly recognized it.

Everts' eyes widened briefly. The man bowed faintly. "Thank you, Dr. Feldman."

It was ridiculous, impossible, and yet there was a curious relief at the formality of it. It was like something from a play, too unreal to affect his life.

Everts nodded to the man holding the helmet. Doc dropped his bracky weed and felt the helmet snap down. A hiss of oxygen reached him and the suit ballooned out. There was no gravity; the two men handed him up easily to the one in the airlock while the inner seal began to close.

There was still ten seconds to go, according to the big chronometer that had been installed in the lock. The spaceman used it in tying the sack of possessions firmly to Doc's suit.

A red light went on. The man caught Doc and held him against the outer seal. The red light blinked. Four seconds...three...two...

There was a sudden heavy thudding sound, and the *Iroquois* seemed to jerk sideways slightly. The spaceman's face swung around in surprise.

The red light blinked and stayed on. Zero!

The outer seal snapped open and the spaceman heaved. Air exploded outwards, and Doc went with it. He was alone in space, gliding away from the ship, with oxygen hissing softly through the valve and ticking away his life.

CHAPTER ELEVEN
Convert

Feldman fought for control of himself, forced himself to think, to hold onto his sanity. It was sheer stupidity, since nothing could have been more merciful than to lose this reality. But the will to be himself was stronger than logic. And bit by bit, he forced the fear and horror away from him until he could examine his situation.

He was spinning slowly, so that stars ahead of him seemed to crawl across his view. The ship was retreating from him already hundreds of yards away. Mars was a shrunken pill far away.

Then something blinked to one side. He turned his head to stare.

A little ship was less than three hundred yards away. He recognized it as a life raft. Now his spin brought him around to face it, and he saw it was parallelling his course. The ejection of the life raft must have caused the thump he'd heard before he was cast adrift.

It meant someone was trying to save him. It meant *life*!

He flailed his arms and beat his legs together, senselessly trying to force himself closer, while trying to guess who could have taken the chance. No one he could think of could have booked passage on the *Iroquois*. There wasn't that much free money in the villages.

Something flashed a hot blue, and the little ship leaped forward. Whoever was handling it knew nothing about piloting. It picked up too much speed at too great an angle.

Again blue spurts came, but this time matters were even worse. Then there was a long wait before a third try was made. He estimated the course. It would miss him by a good hundred feet, but it was probably the best the amateur pilot could do. The ship drifted closer, but to one side. It would soon pass him completely.

A spacesuited figure suddenly appeared in the tiny airlock, holding a coil of rope. The rope shot out, well thrown. But it was too short. It would pass within ten feet—and might as well have been ten miles for all the good it would do him.

Every film he had seen on space seemed to form a mad jumble in his mind, but he seized on the first idea he could remember. He inhaled deeply and yanked the oxygen tank free. An automatic seal on the suit cut off the connection. He aimed the hissing bottle, fumbling for the manual valve.

It almost worked. It kicked him toward the rope slightly, but most of the energy was wasted in setting him into a wilder spin. He blinked, trying to spot the rope. It was within five feet now.

Again he waited, until he seemed to be in position. This time he threw the bottle away from it. It added spin to his vertical axis, but the rope came into view within arm's reach.

He grasped it, just as his lungs seemed about to burst. He couldn't hold on long enough to tie the rope...

His lungs gave up suddenly, collapsing and then sucking in greedily. Clean air rushed in, letting his head clear. He'd forgotten that the inflated suit held enough oxygen for several minutes.

His body struck the edge of the airlock and a hand jerked him inside. The outer seal was slammed shut and locked, and there was a hiss of air entering.

He threw back his helmet just as Chris Ryan jerked hers off.

Her voice shook almost hysterically. "Thank God. Dan, I almost gave up!"

"I liked the air out there better," he told her bitterly. "If you'll open the lock again, I'll leave. Or am I supposed to believe this is rescue and that you came along just to save me?"

"I came along to see you killed, as you know very well. Saving you wasn't in my orders."

He grunted and reached for the handle that would release the outer lock. "Better get back inside if you don't want to blow out with me."

"It's up to you, Dan," she told him, and there was all the sincerity in the world in her blue eyes. "I'm on your side now."

He began counting on his fingers. "Let's see. The spare battery, the delay in arresting me, the choice of Matthews—"

"It was all true." Anger began to grow in her eyes. "Dan Feldman, you get inside this raft! If you don't care about me, you might consider the people dying of the plague who need you!"

She'd played her trump, and it took the round. He followed her.

"All right," he said grudgingly. "Spill your story."

She held out a copy of a space radiogram, addressed to Mrs. D. E. Everts, and signed by one of the best doctors on the Lobby Board of Directors.

Regret confirm diagnosis. Topsecret. Repeat topsecret. Martian fever incubates fourteen years, believed highly fatal. No cure, research beginning immediately. Penalty violation topsecret, death all concerned.

"Mrs. Everts rates a topsecret break?" Doc commented dryly. "Come off it, Chris!"

"She's the daughter of Elmers of Space Lobby!" Chris answered. She pointed to the message, underlining words with her finger. "*Fourteen years.* You couldn't have caused it. *Highly fatal.* And people are being told it's only a skin disease.

Research beginning. But you've already done most of the research. I can see that now. I can see a lot of things."

"You've got me beat then," he said. "I can't see how such a reformed young noblewoman calmly walked over and stole a life raft. I can't see how your brilliant mind concocted this whole scheme in almost no time. And to be honest, I can't even see why Medical Lobby decided to save me at the last minute and sent you to do the job. You didn't have to spy out knowledge from me. I've been trying all along to get it to your Research division."

She sighed and dropped onto a little seat.

"I can't prove my motives. You'll just have to believe me. But it wasn't hard to do what I've done. That shuttle pilot was found in a routine check, stowed away on the life raft. I was with Captain Everts when he was found, so I discovered how to get into the raft. And I heard his whole confession. He wasn't the real pilot. He'd come from the villages to save you. The whole scheme was his. I just used it, hoping I could reach you."

As always her story had a convincing element she shouldn't have known. The pilot's farewell, addressing him as Dr. Feldman, had been too low for her to hear, but it was something that fitted her story. It was probably a deliberate clue to give him hope, to assure him the villages were still trying. It shook his confidence.

"And your motive—your real motive?" he insisted.

She swore at him, then began ripping off the spacesuit. She turned her back, pulling a thin blouse down from her neck. He stared, then reached out to touch the lump there.

"So you've had Selznik's migraine and know you're carrying plague. And you've decided your precious Lobby won't save you?"

She dropped her eyes, then raised them to meet his defiantly. "I'm not just scared and selfish. Dad caught it, too, and it must be close to the time for him. He switched to Mars-normal when he was a liaison agent and never changed back. Dan, are we all going to have to die? Can't you save him?"

Feldman was out of his suit and at the control panel. There was a manual lever, which Chris must have used before. It might work out here where there was room to maneuver and nothing to hit. But trying to make a landing was going to be different.

"Dan?" she repeated.

He shrugged. "I don't know. They've started research too late and they'll be under so much pressure that the real brains won't have a chance. The topsecret stuff looks bad for research. Maybe there's a cure. It works in culture bottles, but it may fail in person. When I'm convinced I'm safe with you, I may tell you about it."

"Oh." Her voice was low. Then she sighed. "I suppose I can understand why you hate me, Dan."

"I don't hate you. I'm too mixed up. Tomorrow maybe, but not now. Shut up and let me see if I can figure out how to land this thing."

He found that the fuel tanks were nearly full, but that still didn't leave much margin. Mars must have been notified by Everts and be ready to pick the raft up. He had to reach the wastelands away from any of the shuttle ports. They had no aspirators, however, and they couldn't cover much territory in the spacesuits they would have to use. It meant he'd have to land close to a village where he was known.

He jockeyed the ship around by trial and error, studying the manual that was lying prominently on the control panel. According to the booklet, the ship was simple to operate. It was self-leveling in an atmosphere, and automatic flare computers were supposed to make it possible for an amateur to judge the rate of descent near the surface. It looked reassuring—and was probably written with that in mind.

Finally he reached for the control, hoping he'd figured his landing orbit reasonably well by simple logic. He smoothed it out in the following hours as he watched the markings on Mars. When they were near turnover point, he began cranking the little gyroscope to swing the ship. It saved fuel to turn without power, and he wasn't sure he could have turned accurately by blasting.

He was gaining some proficiency, however, he felt. But now he had to waste fuel and ruin his orbit again. There was no way to practice maneuvering without actually doing so.

In the end, he compromised, leaving a small margin for a bad landing that would require a second attempt, but with less practice than he wanted.

He had located Jake's village through the little telescope when he finally reached for the main blast control. The thin haze of Mars' atmosphere came rushing up, while the blast lashed out. Then they were in the outer fringes of the sky and the blast was beginning to show a corona that ruined visibility.

He turned to the flare computer and back to what he could see through the quartz viewport. He was going to land about half a mile from the village, as nearly as he could judge.

The computer seemed to work as it should. The speed was within acceptable limits. He gave up trying to see the ground and was forced to trust the machinery designed for amateur pilots. The flare bloomed, and he yanked down on the little lever.

It could have been worse. They hit the ground, bounced twice, and turned over. The ship was a mess when Feldman freed himself from the elastic straps of the seat. Chris had shrieked as they hit, but she was unbuckling herself now.

He threw her her spacesuit and one of the emergency bottles of oxygen from the rack. "Hurry up with that. We've sprung a leak and the pressure's dropping."

They were halfway to the village when a dozen tractors came racing up and Jake piled out of the lead one to drag the two in with him.

"Heard about it from the broadcasts and figured you might land around here. Good to see you, Doc." He started the tractor off at full speed, back to the wastelands, while Doc stared at the armed men who were riding the tractors.

Jake caught his look and nodded. "You're in enemy territory, Doc. There's a war going on!"

CHAPTER TWELVE
War

Sometimes it seemed to Doc that war was nothing but an endurance race to see how many times they could run before they were bombed. He was just beginning to drop off to sleep after a long trip for the sixth consecutive day when the little alarm shrilled. He sighed and shook Chris awake.

"Again?" she protested. But she got up and began helping him pack.

Jake came in, his eyes weary, pulling on the old jacket with the big star on its sleeve. Doc hadn't been too surprised to learn that Jake was the actual leader of the rebels. "Shuttles spotted taking off this way. And I still can't find where the leak is. They haven't missed our location once this week. Here, give me that."

He took the electron mike that had been among Doc's' possessions, but Chris recaptured it. "I can manage," she told him, and headed out for the tractor where Lou was waiting.

Doc scowled after her. He and Jake had been watching her. She was too useful to Doc's research to be turned away, but they didn't trust her yet. So far, however, they had found nothing wrong with her conduct. Still...

He swung suddenly into Jake's tractor. "Just remembered something. How'd they find me that time I stopped in the tractor to use the mike? I was pretty well hidden, and no tracks last in the sand long enough for them to have followed. But they were there when I came to. Somehow, they must have put a radio tracer on me."

Jake waited while they lighted up, his eyes suddenly bright. "You mean something you got from her house was bugged? It figures."

"And I've still got all the stuff. Now they find wherever we set up headquarters, though they've always managed to miss my laboratory, even when they've hit the troops around us. Jake, I think it's the microscope." Doc managed to push enough junk off one of the seats to make a cramped bed, and stretched out. "Sure, we figured they sent her because they want to keep tabs on what I discover. They've finally gotten scared of the plague, and she's the perfect Judas goat. But they have to have some way to get in touch with her. I'll bet there's a tracer in the mike and a switch so she can modulate it or key it to send out Morse."

"Yeah," Jake nodded. "Well, she does her own dirty work. I might get to like her if she was on our side. Okay, Doc. If they've put things into the mike, I've got a boy who'll find and fix it so she won't guess it's been touched."

Doc relaxed. For the moment, there would be no power in the instrument, nor any excuse for her to use it. But she must have handled some secret arrangement during the work periods. She used the mike more than he did. The switch could be camouflaged easily enough. If anyone detected the signal, they'd probably only think it was some leak in the electrical circuit.

Far away, the shuttle rockets had appeared as tiny dots in the sky. They were standing on their tails a second later, just off the ground, letting the full force of their blasts bake the area where headquarters had been.

Jake watched grimly, driving by something close to instinct. Then he looked back. "Know anything about a Dr. Harkness?"

"Not much, except that he protested sealing off the villages. Why?"

"He and five other doctors were picked up, trying to get through to us. Claimed they wanted to give us medical help. We can use them, God knows. I guess I'll have to chance it."

They stopped at a halfway village and hid the tractors before looking for a place to rest. Doc found Chris curled up asleep against the microscope. He had a hard time getting her to leave it in the tractor, but she was too genuinely tired to put up any real argument.

Jake reported in the morning before they set out again. "You were right, Doc. It was a nice job of work. Must have taken the best guys in Southport to hide the circuit so well. But it's safe now. It just makes a kind of meaningless static nobody can trace. Maybe we can get you a permanent lab now."

Doc debated again having Chris left behind and decided against it. The Lobby was determined to let him find a cure for them if he could. That meant Chris would work herself to exhaustion trying to help. Let her think she was doing it for the Lobby! It was time she was on the receiving end of a double cross.

"It's a stinking way to run a war," he decided.

Jake chuckled without much humor. "It's the war you wanted, remember? They forced our hand, but it had to come sometime. Right now the Lobby's fighting to get their hands on your work before we can use it; they're just using holding tactics, which helps our side. And we're hoping you get the cure so we can win. With that, maybe we'll whip them."

It was a crazy war, with each side killing more of its own men than of the enemy. The runners were increasing, and Jake's army was learning to shoot the poor devils mercifully and go on. They knew, at least, that there was no current danger of infection. In the Lobby towns, more were dying of panic in their efforts to escape the runners.

Desert towns had joined the villages, reluctantly but inevitably, to give the rebels nearly three-quarters of the total population. But the Lobby forces and the few cities held most of the real fighting equipment and they were ready to wait until Earth could send out unmanned rockets, loaded with atomics, which could cut through space at ten times normal speed.

There were vague lines of battle, but time was the vital factor. The Lobbies waited to steal a cure for the plague and the villages waited until they could announce it and demand surrender as its price.

It looked as if both sides were doomed to disappointment, however. He and Chris had put in every spare minute between moving and the minimum of sleep in searching for something that would check the disease. It couldn't grow in an Earth-normal body, but it didn't die, either. And there wasn't enough normal food available to permit the switch-over for more than a handful of people. Even Earth was out of luck, since eighty percent of her population ate synthetics. There were ways to synthesize Earth-normal food, but they were still hopelessly inefficient.

Jake had ordered one of the villages to rebuild their plant for such a purpose, while another was producing the enzyme that would permit switching. But it looked hopeless for more than a few of the most valuable men.

"No progress?" Jake asked for the hundredth time.

Doc grinned wryly. "A lot, but no help. We've found a fine accelerator for the bug. We can speed up its incubation or even make someone already infected catch it all over again. But we can't slow it down or stop it."

The new laboratory was still being fitted when they arrived. It had been dug into one of the few real cliffs in this section of Mars. The power plant had been installed, complete with a steam plant that would operate off sunlight in the daytime through a series of heat valves that took in a lot of warm air and produced smaller amounts hot enough to boil water.

"I'll see you whenever I can," Jake said. "But mostly, you're going to be somewhat isolated so they won't trace you. Let them think they goofed with the shuttles and hit you and Chris. Anything you need?"

"Guinea pigs," Doc told him sarcastically. It was meant as a joke, though a highly bitter one. Jake nodded and left them.

Doc opened the cots as Chris came in, not bothering to unpack the equipment. "Hit the sack, Chris," he told her.

She looked at him doubtfully. "You almost said that the way you'd address a human being, Dan. You're slipping. One of these days you'll like me again."

"Maybe." He was too tired to argue. "I doubt it, though. Forget it and get some sleep."

She watched him silently until he got up to turn out the light. Then she sighed heavily. "Dan?"

"Yeah?"

"I never got a divorce. The publicity would have been bad. But anyway, we're still married."

"That's nice." He swung to face her briefly. "And they found the radio in the microscope. Better get to sleep, Chris."

"Oh." It was a quiet exclamation, barely audible. There was a sound that might have been a sniffle if it had come from anyone else. Then she rolled over. "All right, Dan. I still want to help you."

He cursed himself for a stupid fool for telling her. Fatigue was ruining what judgment he had. From now on, he'd have to watch her every minute. Or had she really seen the value of the research by now? She wasn't a fool. It should have registered on even her stubborn mind. But he was too sleepy to think about it.

She had breakfast ready in the morning. She made no comment on what had been said during the night. Instead, she began discussing a way to keep one of the organic antibiotics from splitting into simpler compounds when they tried to switch it over to Mars-normal. They were both hopelessly bad chemists and biologists, but there was no one else to do the work.

Chris worked harder than ever during the day.

Just after sundown, Jake came in with a heavy box. He dropped it onto the floor. "Mice!"

Doc ripped off the cover, exposing fine screening. There were at least six dozen mice inside!

"Harkness found them," Jake explained. "A hormone extraction plant used them for testing some of the products. Had them sent by regular shipments from Earth. Getting them cost a couple of men, but Harkness claims it's worth it. He's a good man on a raid. Here!"

He'd gone to the doorway again and came back with another box, this one crammed with bottles and boxes. "They had quite a laboratory, and Harkness picked out whatever he thought you could use."

Chris and Doc were going through it. The labels were engineering ones, but the chemical formulae were identification enough. There were dozens of chemicals they hadn't hoped to get.

"Anything else?" Doc finally asked as they began arranging the supplies.

"More runners. A lot more. We're still holding things down, but it's reaching a limit. Panic will start in the camps if this keeps on. But that's my worry. You stick to yours."

Several of the new chemicals showed promise in the tubes. But two of them proved fatal to the mice and the others were completely innocuous in the little animal's bodies, both to mouse and to germ. The plague was much hardier in contact with living cells than in the artificial environment of the culture jars.

They lost seven mice in two days, but that seemed unimportant; the females were already living up to their reputations, nearly all pregnant. Doc didn't know the gestation period, but he remembered that it was short.

"Funny they all started at the same time," he commented. "Must have been shipped out separately or else been kept apart while they were switched over to Mars-normal. Something interrupted their habits, anyhow."

A few nights later they learned what it was. There was a horrible squealing that woke him out of the depths of his sleep. Chris was already at the light switch. As light came on, they turned to the mouse box.

All the animals were charging about in their limited space, their little legs driving madly and their mouths open. What they lacked in size they made up in numbers, and the din was terrific.

But it didn't last. One by one, the mice began dropping to the floor of the cage. In fifteen minutes, they were all dead!

It was obviously the plague, contracted after having their metabolism switched. Women were sterile for some time after Selznik's migraine struck, and the same must have been true of the mice. They must have contracted the plague at about the same time and reached fertility together. Somehow, the plague incubation period had been shortened to fit their life span; the disease was nothing if not adaptive.

Chris prepared a slide in dull silence. The familiar cell was there when Doc looked through the microscope. He picked up one of the little creatures and cut it open, removing one of the foetuses.

"Make a film of that," he suggested.

She worked rapidly, scraping out the almost microscopic brain, dissolving out the fatty substance, and transferring the result to a film. This time, even at full magnification, there was no sign of the filaments that were always present in diseased flesh. The results were the same for the other samples they made.

"Something about the very young animal or a secretion from the mother's organs keeps the bug from working." Doc reached for a bracky weed and accepted a light from Chris without thinking of it. "Every kid I've heard about contracted the plague between the second and third year. None are born with it, none get it earlier. I've suspected this, but now here's confirmation."

Chris began preparing specimens, while Doc got busy with tubes of the culture. They'd have to test various fluids from the tiny bodies, but there were enough cultures prepared. Then, if the substance only inhibited growth, there would be a long, slow test; if it killed the bugs, they might know more quickly.

Jake came in before the final tests, but waited on them. Doc was studying a film in the microscope. He suddenly motioned excitedly for Chris.

"See the filaments? They're completely disintegrated. And there's one of the big cells broken open. We've got it! It's in the blood of the foetus. And it must be in the blood of newborn children, too!"

Jake looked at the slide, but his face was doubtful.

"Maybe you've got something, Doc. I hope so. And I hope you can use it." He shook his head wearily. "We need good news right now. A couple of big rockets just reached the station and they've been sending shuttles back and forth a mile a minute. Nobody can figure how they got here so fast or what they're for. But it doesn't look good for us!"

CHAPTER THIRTEEN
Susceptibility

Doc could feel the tension in the village where GHQ was temporarily located long before they were close enough for details to register. The people were gathered in clusters, staring at the sky where the station must be. A few were pacing up and down, gesticulating with tight sweeps of their arms.

One woman suddenly went into even more violent action. She leaped into the air and then took off at a rapid trot, then a run. Her hands were tearing at her clothes and her mouth seemed to be working violently. She was halfway to the top of the nearest dune before a rifle cracked. She dropped, to twitch once and lie still.

Almost with her death, another figure leaped from one of the houses, his face bare of the necessary aspirator. He took off at a violent run, but he was falling from lack of air before the bullet ended his struggles.

The people suddenly began to move apart, as if trying to get away from each other. For weeks they had faced the horror with courage; now it was finally too much for them.

Tension mounted as no news came from the cities. Doc noticed that it seemed to aggravate or speed up the disease. He saw three men shot in the next half-hour.

He was trying to calm them with word of a possible cure for the plague, but their reactions were as curiously dull as those of Jake had been. As he spoke, they faced him with set expressions. At his mention of the need for the blood of young children, they turned from him, sullenly silent.

Jake came over, nodding unhappily. "It's what I was afraid might happen, Doc. George Lynn! Tell Doc what's wrong."

Lynn was reluctant, but he finally stumbled out his explanation. "It ain't like you, Doc. Comes from that Lobby woman you got. It's her dirty idea. We've seen the Lobby doctors cutting open our kids, poisoning their blood, and bleeding them dry. That ain't gonna happen again, Doc. You tell her it ain't!"

Doc swore as he realized their ignorance. An unexplained vaccination looked like poisoning of the blood. But he couldn't understand the bleeding part until Jake filled him in.

"Northport infant's wing. Each department has its own blood bank and donation is compulsory. Southport started it a couple months ago, too."

The long arm of the Lobby had reached out again. Now if he ever got them to try the treatment, it would be only after long sessions of preparing them with the facts, and there was hardly enough time for the crucial work!

By afternoon, Judge Ben Wilson reached them. His voice shook with fatigue as he climbed up to address the crowd through a power megaphone. "Southport's going crazy." He had to pause for breath between each sentence. "Earth's pulling back all the important people. They're packing them into the ships. They're leaving only colonials with no Earth rights. Those ships left when they decided the plague was coming from here. They won't let anybody back until the plague is licked. There won't be an Earth technician on Mars tomorrow."

"No bombs?" someone called.

"No bombs. The ships must have started before you rebelled, maybe meant honestly to save their own kind. But now it's a military action, and don't think it won't mean trouble. The poor devils in the city bet on the wrong horse.

Now they can't run their food factories or anything else for long. Not without technicians. They've got to whip you now. Up to this time, they've been fighting for the Lobbies. Now they'll fight you for their own bellies to get your supplies. And they've still got shuttle rockets and fuel for them. Now beat it. I gotta confer with Jake."

Doc started after the judge, but Dr. Harkness caught his arm and drew him aside. Chris followed.

"I've found another epidemic," Harkness told them. "Over at Marconi. It's kept me on the run all night, and now half the village is down with it. Starts like a common cold, runs a fair fever, and the skin breaks out all over with bright red dots..."

He went on describing it. Chris began asking him about what medical supplies he had brought with him, pilfered from Northport hospital. She seemed to know what it was, but refused to say until she saw the cases. Doc also preferred to wait. Sometimes things weren't as bad as they seemed, though usually they were worse.

Marconi was dead to all outward appearances, with nobody on the streets. It had been a village of great hopes a week before, since this was where they had decided to experiment with switching the people back to Earth-normal. They'd had the best chance of survival of anyone on Mars until this came up.

Three people lay on the beds in the first house Harkness led them to. The room was darkened, and a man was stumbling around, trying to tend the others, though the little spots showed on his skin. He grinned weakly. "Hi, Doc. I guess we're making a lot of trouble, ain't we?"

Chris gave Doc no chance to answer. "Just as I thought. Measles! Plain old-fashioned measles."

"Figured so," the sick man said. "Like my brother back on Earth."

The others looked doubtful, but Doc reassured them. Chris should know; she'd worked in a swanky hospital where the patients were mostly Earth-normal. Measles was one of the diseases which was foiled by the metabolism switch. Well, at least they wouldn't have to be quarantined here.

Chris finished treating the family with impersonal efficiency, discussing the symptoms loudly with Harkness. "It's a good thing it isn't serious!"

"No," Harkness answered bitterly. "Not serious. It's only killed five children and three adults so far!"

"It would, here," Doc agreed unhappily. He led Chris out of the room on the pretext of washing his hands. "It's serious enough to force us to abandon the whole idea of going back to Earth-normal. Measles today, smallpox, tuberculosis, scarlet fever and everything else tomorrow. These people have lived Mars-normal so long their natural immunity has been destroyed. On Earth where the disease was everywhere, kids used to pick up some immunity with constant exposure, even without what might be called a case of the disease. Here, the blood has no reason to build antibodies. They can be killed by things people used to laugh at. How the disease got here, I don't know. But it's here. So we'll have to give up the idea of switching back to Earth-normal."

He gathered up one of the kits and started toward the other houses. "And Lord knows how long it will take to get the blood for the other treatment, even if it works."

They worked as a team for a while, with Harkness frowning as he watched Chris. Finally the young doctor stopped Chris outside the fifth house. "These are my patients, Dr. Ryan. I left the Lobby because I didn't believe colonials were mere livestock. I still feel the same. I appreciate your help in diagnosis and methods of treatment. But I can't let you handle my patients this way."

"Dan!" She swung around with eyes glazing. "Dan, are you going to stand for that?"

"I think you'd better wait in the tractor, Chris."

He was lucky enough to catch the kit she threw at him before its precious contents spilled. But it wasn't luck that guided his hand to the back of her skirt hard enough to leave it stinging.

Her face froze and she stormed out. A moment later they heard the tractor start off.

But Doc had no time to think of her. He and Harkness split up and began covering the streets, house by house, while he passed on the word to abandon the metabolism switch and go back to Mars-normal.

Jake sent two other doctors to relieve them late in the evening. Things were somewhat quieter at GHQ as Doc reported the events at Marconi.

"Where's Dr. Ryan?" Jake asked at last.

Doc exchanged glances with Harkness. "She isn't in the lab?"

"Wasn't there an hour ago."

Doc cursed himself for letting her go. With the knowledge that the radio in the mike was disabled, she'd obviously grabbed the first chance to report back. And with her had gone news of the only cure they had found.

Jake took it as philosophically as he could, though it was a heavy blow to his hopes. They spent half the night looking for her tractor, on the chance that she might have gotten lost or broken down, but there was no sign of it.

She was waiting in the laboratory when he returned at dawn. Her face was dirty and her uniform was a mess. But she was smiling. She got up to greet him, holding out two large bottles.

"Infant plasma—straight from Southport. And if you think I had it easy lying my way in and out of the hospital, you're a fool, Dan Feldman. If the man who took my place there hadn't been a native idiot, I never would have gotten away with it."

The things he had suspected could still be right, he realized. She could have reported everything to the Lobby. It was a better explanation than her vague account of bullying her way in and out. But she'd had a rough drive, and he wanted the plasma. Curiously, he was glad to have her back with him. He reached out a hand for the bottles.

She put the bottle on the table and grabbed up a short-bladed knife. "Not so fast," she cried. Her eyes were blazing now. "Dan Feldman, if you touch those bottles until you've crawled across the floor on your face and apologized for the way you treated me the last few days, I'll cut your damned heart out."

He shook his head, chuckling at the picture she made. There were times when he could almost see why he'd married her.

"All right, Chris," he gave in. "I'll be darned if I'll crawl, but you've earned an apology. Okay?"

She sighed uncertainly. Then she nodded and began changing for work.

CHAPTER FOURTEEN
Immunity

They worked through the day in what seemed to be armed truce. There was no coffee waiting for him when he awoke next, as he'd come to expect, but he didn't comment. He went to where she was already working, checking on the results of the plasma on the cultures.

The response had been slower than with the mouse blood, but now the bugs seemed to be dead. The filaments were destroyed, and there were no signs of the big cells. It seemed to be a cure, at least in the culture bottles.

"We'll need volunteers," he decided. "There should be animals, but we don't have any. At least this stuff isn't toxic. We need a natural immune and someone infected. Two of each, so one can be treated and the other used for a control. Makes four. Not enough to be sure, but it will have to do."

"Two," Chris corrected. "You're not infected, I am."

"Two others," he agreed. "I'll get them from Jake."

Most of GHQ was out on the street, but Doc found Jake inside the big schoolroom where he enjoyed his early morning bracky and coffee. The chief listened and agreed at once, turning to the others in the room.

"Who's had the jumping headache? Okay, Swanee. Who never had it?" He blinked in surprise as three men nodded out of the eight present. "I guess you go, Tom."

The two men stood up, tamping out their weeds, and went out with Doc.

Chris had everything set up. They matched coins to decide who would be treated. Doc noticed that Chris would get no plasma, while he was scheduled for everything. He watched her prepare the culture and add the accelerator that would speed development and make certain he and Tom were infected, then let her inject it.

That was all, except for the waiting. To keep conditions more closely alike, they were to stay there until the tests were finished, not even eating for fear of upsetting the conditions. Swanee dug out a pack of worn cards and began to deal while Doc dug out some large pills to use as chips.

It was an hour later when the pain began. Doc had just won the pot of fifty pills and opened his mouth for the expected gloating. He yelled as an explosion seemed to go off inside his head. Even closing his mouth was agony.

A moment later, Tom began to sweat. It got worse, spreading to the whole area of the back of the head and neck. Doc lay on the cot, envying Chris and Swanee who had already been infected naturally. He longed desperately for bracky, and had to keep reminding himself that no drugs must upset the tests. It was the longest day he had ever spent, and he began to doubt that he could get through it. He watched the little clock move from one minute to nine over to half a minute and hung breathless until it hit the nine. There was no question about whether the infection had taken. Now they could dull the agony.

Chris had the anodyne tablets already dissolved in water, and Swanee was passing out three lighted bracky weeds. It took a few minutes for the relief of the anodyne, and even that couldn't kill all the pain. But it didn't matter by comparison. He sucked the weed, mashed it out and began dealing the cards again.

They had a plentiful supply of the anodyne and used it liberally during the night. The test was a speeded-up simulation of the natural course of the disease, where painkiller would take time to get for most people here, but would then be used generously.

Precisely at nine in the morning, Chris began to inject Swanee and Doc with plasma.

Now there was no thought of cards. They waited, trying to talk, but with most of their attention on the clock. Doc had estimated that an hour should be enough to show results, but it was hard to remember that an hour was the guess as to the minimum time.

He winced as Chris took a tiny bit of flesh from his neck. She went to the other men, and then submitted to his work on herself. Then she began preparing the slides.

"Feldman," she read the name of the slide as she inserted it into the microscope. Then her breath caught sharply. "Only dead cells!"

It was the same for Swanee and Tom. Each had to look at his own slide and have it explained before the results could be believed. But at last Chris bent over her own slide. A minute later she glanced up, nodding. "What it should be. It checks."

Tom whooped and went out the door to notify Jake. There was only plasma for some two hundred injections, but that should yield sufficient proof. Once salvation was offered, there should be no trouble convincing the people that blood donations from their children were worthwhile.

Later, when the last of the plasma had been used, they could finally relax. Chris slipped off her smock and dropped onto the cot. A tired smile came onto her lips. "You're forgiven, Dan," she said. A moment later she was obviously asleep. Doc meant to join her, but it was too much effort. He leaned his head forward onto his arms, vaguely wondering why she was calling off the feud.

It was night outside when he awoke, and he was lying on the cot, though he still felt cramped and strained. He stirred, groaning, and finally realized that a hand was on his shoulder shaking him. He looked up to see Jake above him. Chris was busy with the coffee maker.

Jake slumped onto the cot beside Doc. "We took Southport," he announced.

That knocked the sleep out of Doc's system. "You what?"

"We took it, lock, stock and barrel. I figured the news of your cure would put guts into the men, and it did. But we'd probably have taken it anyhow. There wasn't anything to fight for there after Earth pulled out and the plague really hit. Wilson mistook last-minute panic for fighting spirit. The poor devils didn't have anything to fight about, once the Lobby stopped goading them."

Doc tried to assimilate the news. But once the surprise was gone, he found it meant very little. Maybe his revolutionary zeal had cooled, once the Lobby men had pulled out. "We'll need a lot more plasma than there is in Southport," he said.

"Not so much, maybe," Jake denied. "Doc, three of the men you injected were shot down as runners. Your plasma's no good."

"It takes time to work, Jake. I told you there might be a case or two that would be too close to the edge. Three is more than I expected; but it's not impossible."

"There was plenty of time. They blew after we got back from Southport." Jack dropped his hand on Doc's shoulder, and his face softened. "Harkness tested every man you injected. He finished half an hour ago. Five showed dead bugs. The rest of them weren't helped at all."

Doc fumbled for a weed, trying to think. But his thoughts refused to focus. "Five!"

"Five out of two hundred. That's about average. And what about Tom? He was jumping around after the test last night, telling how you'd cured him, how he'd seen the dead bugs; but he never had the jumping headache, and you never gave him the plasma! He's got dead bugs, though. Harkness tested him."

Doc let his realization of his own idiocy sink in until he could believe it. Jake was right. Tom had never been treated, yet Chris had reported dead bugs. They'd all been so ready to believe in miracles that no one had been able to think straight after the long wait.

"There was a bump on his neck—a small one," he said slowly. "Jake, he must have caught it, even if he seemed immune. If he was taking anodyne anyway for something—or unconscious—"

"He was up in Northport six years ago for a kidney operation," Jake admitted doubtfully. "We had to chip in to pay for it. But you still didn't treat him, and he's cured. Face it, Doc, that plasma is no good inside the body."

His hand tightened on Doc's shoulder again. "We're not blaming you. We don't judge a man here except by what he is. Maybe the stuff helps a little. We'll go on using it when we get it; tell everybody you were a mite optimistic, so they'll figure it's a gamble, but have a little hope left. And you keep trying. Something cured it in Tom. Now you find out what."

Doc watched him go out numbly, and turned to Chris.

"It can't be right," she said shakily. "You and Swanee were cured. Maybe it was the accelerator. It had to be something."

"You didn't have the accelerator," he accused.

"No, and I've still got live bugs. I was never supposed to be cured, so I expected to see just what I saw. How I missed the fact that Tom should have been like me, I don't know. Damn it, oh, damn it!"

He's never seen her cry before, except in fury. But she mastered it almost at once, shaking tears out of her eyes. "All right. Plasma works in a bottle but not in an adult body. Maybe something works in the body but not in a bottle."

"Maybe. And maybe some people are just naturally immune after it reaches a certain stage. Maybe we ran into coincidence."

But he didn't believe that, any more than she did. The answer had to be in the room. He'd taken a massive dose of the disease and been cured in a few hours.

Outside the room, the war went on, drawing toward a close. The supposed partial cure was good propaganda, if nothing else, and Jake was widening his territory steadily. There was only token resistance against him. He had the Southport shuttles now to cover huge areas in a hurry. But inside the room, the battle was less successful. It wasn't the accelerator. It wasn't the tablets of anodyne. They even tried sweeping the floor and using the dust without results.

Then another test in the room, made with four volunteers Jake selected, yielded complete cures after injections with plain salt water in place of plasma.

The plague speeded up again. About four people out of a hundred now seemed to have caught the disease and cured themselves. They accounted for what faith was left in Doc's plasma and gave some unfounded hope to the others.

Northport fell a week later, putting the whole planet in rebel hands.

Jake returned, wearier than ever. He'd proved to be one of the natural immunes, but the weight of the campaign that could only end in a defeat by the plague left him no room to rejoice in his personal fortune.

This time he looked completely defeated. And a moment later, Doc saw why as Jake flipped a flimsy sheet onto the table. It bore the seals of Space and Medical Lobbies.

Jake pointed upwards. "The war rockets are there, all right. We knew they'd come. Now all they want for calling them off is our surrender and your cure. If they don't get both, they'll blow the planet to bits. We have two days."

The rockets could be seen clearly with binoculars. There were more than enough to destroy all life on the planet. Maybe they'd be used eventually, anyhow, since the Lobbies wanted no more rebellion. But with a cure for the plague, he might have bought them off.

Chris stood beside him, looking as if it were a bitter pill for her, too. She'd risked herself in the hands of the enemy, had cooperated with him in everything she'd been taught to oppose, and had worked like a dog. Now the Lobbies seemed to forget her as a useless tool. They were falling back on a raw power play and forgetting any earlier schemes.

"Maybe they'd hold off for a while if I agreed to go to them and share all my ideas, specimens and notes," he said at last. "Do you think your Lobby would settle for that, Chris?"

"I don't know, Dan. I've stopped thinking their way." She seemed almost apologetic for the admission.

He dropped an arm over her shoulder and turned with her back to the laboratory. "Okay, then we've got to find a miracle. We've got two days ahead of us. At least we can try."

But he knew he was lying to himself. There wasn't anything he could think of to try.

CHAPTER FIFTEEN
Decision

Two days was never enough time for a miracle. Doc decided as he packed his notes into a small bag and put it beside his bundle of personal belongings. He glanced around the room for the last time, and managed a grin at Jake's gloomy expression.

"Maybe I can bluff them, or maybe they'll string along for a while," he said. "Anyhow, now that they've agreed to take me and my notes in place of the cure we're fresh out of, I've got to be on that shuttle when it goes back to their men at orbital station."

Jake nodded. "I don't like selling friends down the river, Doc. But it wouldn't do you any more good to blow up with the planet, I reckon. They won't call off the war rockets when they do get you, of course. But maybe they won't use them, except as a threat to put the Lobbies back in, stronger than ever."

He stuck out one of his awkwardly shaped hands, clapped the aspirator over his face and hurried out. Doc picked up his bags and went toward the little tractor where Lou was waiting to drive him and Chris back toward Southport and the shuttle rocket that would be landing for them. They hadn't mentioned Chris in their demands, but her father must expect her to return.

After they had him, he'd be on his own. His best course was probably to insist on talking only to Ryan at Medical Lobby, and then being completely honest. The room here would be kept sealed, in case the Lobby wanted to investigate where he had failed. And his notes were honest, which was something that could usually be determined. Chris could testify to that, anyhow, since she'd kept a lot of them for him.

At best, there would be a chance for some compromise and perhaps some clue for them that might eventually end the plague. They had enough men to work on it, and billions in equipment. At worst, he should gain a little time.

"Cheer up, Chris," he told her as he climbed through the little airlock. "Maybe Harkness will turn up the cure before our negotiations break down. He has the whole of Northport Hospital to play with. They haven't tried to chase him out of there yet. After all, we almost found something with no equipment except wild imaginations."

She shook her head as the tractor began moving. "Shut up! I've got enough trouble without your coming down with logorrhea. Don't be a fool."

"Why change now?" he asked her. "Everything I've done has been because I am a fool. I guess my luck lasted longer than I could expect. And I'm still fool enough to think that the solution has to turn up eventually. We know it has to be in that room. Damn it, we must know it—if we could only think straight now."

She reached over and touched his hand, but made no comment. They had been over that statement of desperation too many times already. But it kept nagging at him— something in the room, something in the room! Something so common that nobody noticed it!

They passed a crowd chasing down a runner. Something in that room could have saved the unlucky man. It could have saved Mars, perhaps.

He growled for the hundredth time, cursing his fatigue-numbed mind. Too little sleep, too much coffee and bracky...

He reached for the package of weed, realizing that he would miss it on Earth, if he ever got there. Like everything here on the planet, he'd begun by detesting it and wound up finding it the thing he wanted to keep forever. He lighted the bracky and sat smoking, watching Lou drive. When the first was finished, he lighted another from the butt.

She put out a hand and took it away. "Please, Dan. I can stand the stuff, but I'll never like it, and the tractor's stuffy enough already. I've taken enough of it. And it keeps reminding me of our test—the three of you stinking up the place, puffing and blowing that out, while I couldn't even get a breath of air…"

She was getting logorrhea herself now and—

The answer finally hit him! He jerked around, making a grab for Lou's shoulder, motioning for the man to head back.

"Bracky—it has to be! Chris, that's it. Jake picked out the second group of men from his friends—and they are all cronies because they hang around so much in their so-called smoking room. The first time, it killed the bugs for all of us who smoked—and it didn't work for you because you never learned the habit."

Lou had the tractor turned and the rheostat all the way to the floor.

She was sitting up now, but she wasn't fully satisfied. "The percentage of immunes seems about right. But why do some of the smokers get the disease while some don't?"

"Why not? It depends on whether they pick up the habit before or after the disease gets started. Tom must have got his while he was in Northport. They wouldn't let him smoke there—if he had the habit before, for that matter."

She found no fault with that. He twisted it back and forth in his mind, trying to find a fault. There seemed to be none. The only trouble was that they couldn't send a message that bracky was the cure and hope that Earth would prove it true. No polite note of apology would do after that. They had to be sure. Too many other ideas had proved wrong already.

Jake saw them coming and came running toward the laboratory, but Lou stopped the tractor before it reached the building and let the older man in.

"Get me a dozen men who have the plague. I want the worst cases you have, and ones that Harkness tested himself," Doc ordered. "And then start praying that the cure we've got works fast."

Chris was at the electron mike at once, but one of her hands reached out for the weed. She began puffing valiantly, making sick faces. Now other men began coming in, their faces struggling to find hope, but not daring to believe yet. Jake followed them.

"We'll test at ten-minute intervals. That will be about two hours for the last from the group," Doc decided. One of the doctors Harkness had brought to the villages was busy cutting tiny sections from the lumps on the men's necks, while Chris ran them through the microscope to make sure the bugs were still alive. The regular optical mike was strong enough for that.

Doc handed each man a bracky weed, with instructions to keep smoking, no matter how sick it made him.

There were no results at the end of ten minutes when the first test was made. The second, at the end of twenty minutes, was still infected with live bugs. At the half-hour, Chris frowned.

"I can't be sure—take a look, Dan."

He bent over, moving the slide to examine another spot. "I think so. The next one should tell."

There was no doubt about the fourth test. The bugs were dead, without a single exception that they could find.

One by one, the men were tested and went storming out, shouting the news. For a minute, the gathering crowd was skeptical, remembering the other failures. Then, abruptly, men were screaming, crying and fighting for the precious bracky, like the legions of the damned grabbing for lottery tickets when the prize was a passport to paradise.

Jake swore as he moved toward the door. "We're low on bracky here. Have to get a supply from Edison, I guess, and cart it to the shuttle. Enough for a sample, and to make them want more. It'll be tough, but we'll get it there in time—by the time the shuttle should be picking you up. Doc, you've won our war! From now on, if Earth wants to keep her population up, we'll be a free planet!"

Chris turned slowly from the microscope, holding a slide in her hands. "My bugs," she said unbelievingly. "Dan, they're dead!"

Jake patted her shoulder. "That makes it perfect, girl. Now come on. We've got to start celebrating a victory!"

It was the general feeling of most of the heads of the villages when they met the next day in Southport, using the courtroom that had been presided over so long by Judge Ben Wilson. It was victory, and to the victor belonged the spoils. The bracky had gone out to Earth on a converted war rocket that could make the trip in less than two weeks, and one packet had been specially labeled for Captain Everts. But Earth had already confirmed the cure. The small amounts of the herb found in the botanical collections had been enough to satisfy all doubts.

Harkness, Chris and Doc had been fighting against the desire to rob Earth blind that filled most of the men here for hours now. Now they had the backing of Jake and Ben Wilson. And now finally they leaned back, sensing that the argument had been won.

Bargaining was all right in its place, but it had no place in affairs of life and death such as this. They had to see that Earth received all the bracky she needed. It was only right to charge a fair price for it, but they couldn't restrict it by withholding or overcharging. And they could still gain their ends without blackmail.

Martian alkaloids were tricky things, and bracky smoke contained a number of them. It would take Earth at least ten years to discover and synthesize the right one—and it would still probably cost more than it would to import the weed from Mars. As long as the source of that weed was here, and in the hands of the colonials, there would be no danger of Earth's bombing the planet.

Harkness got up to underscore a point Wilson had made. "The plague lived a million years, and it won't disappear now. The jumping headache, or Selznick's migraine, is unpleasant enough to make us reasonably sure that there will be a steady consumption of the weed. Our problem will be to keep the children from using too much of it, probably." He pulled a weed out and lighted it, puckering his face as the smoke bit his tongue. "I'm told that this gets to be an enjoyable habit. If I can believe that, surely you can believe me when I say we don't have to bargain with lives."

The village men were human, and most of them could remember the strain they had been under when they expected those they loved to die at any hour. It had made them crave vengeance, but now as they had a chance to reexamine it, they began to find it harder to impose the horror of any such threat on others. The final vote was almost unanimous.

Doc listened as they wrangled over the wording of the message to Earth, feeling disconnected from it. He passed Chris a bracky and lighted it for her. She took it automatically, smiling as the smoke hit her lungs. It was one thing they had in common now, at least.

Ben Wilson finally read the message.

"To the people of Earth, greetings!

"On behalf of the free people of Mars, I have the honor to announce that this planet hereby declares itself a sovereign and independent world. We shall continue to regard Earth as our mother, and to consider the health and welfare of her people in no way second to our own in matters which affect both planets. We trust that Earth will share this feeling of mutual friendship. We trust that all strains of hostility will be ended. The advantages to each from peaceful commerce make any course other than the most cordial of relations unthinkable.

"We shall consider proof of such friendship an order by Earth to all rockets circling this planet that they shall deliver themselves safely into our hands, in order that we may begin converting them to peaceful purposes for the trade that is to come. In turn, we pledge that all efforts will be made to ensure a prompt delivery of those products most in demand, including the curative bracky plant."

He turned to Doc then. "You want to sign it, Dr. Feldman? Make it as acting president or something, until we can get around to voting you into permanent office."

"You and Jake fight over the job," Doc told him. "No, Ben, I mean it."

He got up and moved out into the outer room, where he could avoid the stares of amazement that were turned to him. He'd never asked for the honor, and he didn't want it.

Chris came with him. Her face was shocked and something was slowly draining out of it as he looked at her.

"Forget it, Chris," he said. "You're going back to Earth. There is nothing for you here."

She hadn't quite given up. "There could be, Dan. You know that."

"No. No, Chris, I don't think there ever can be. You can't find a man strong enough to rule who'll be weak enough to let you rule in his place. It didn't work on Earth, and it won't work here. Forget the dreams you had of what could be done with a new planet. Those are the dreams that made a mess of the old one."

"I'll be back," she told him. "Some day I'll be back."

He shook his head again. "No. You wouldn't like what you find here. Freedom is heady stuff, but you have to have a taste for it. You can't acquire a fondness for it secondhand. And for a while, there's going to be freedom here. Besides, once you get back to Earth, you'll forget what happened here."

She sighed at last. For the first time since he had known her, she seemed to give in completely. And for that brief moment, he loved what she could have been, but never would be.

"All right, Dan," she said quietly. "I can't fight you. I never could, I see now. I'll take the rocket back. What are you going to do?"

He hadn't bothered to think, but he knew the answer. "Research. What else?"

There would be a lot of research done here. It had been suppressed too long, and had piled up a back-pressure that would have to be relieved. And from that research, he suspected, would come the end of the stable oligarchy of Earth. It could never stand against the changes that would be pouring out of Mars.

She put her hands on his shoulders and moved forward to kiss him. He bent down to meet her, and found her eyes were wet. Maybe his were, too. Then she broke free.

"You're a fool, Dan Feldman," she whispered, and began moving down the hallway and out of the council hall of Mars.

Doc Feldman nodded slowly as he let her go. He was a fool. He had always been a fool, and always would be. And that was why he could never take over leadership here. Fools and idealists should never govern a world. It took practical men such as Jake to do that.

But the practical men needed the foolish idealists, too. And maybe for a time here on Mars their kind of men and his kind of fools could make one more stab at the ancient puzzle of freedom.

Outside the war rockets of Earth began landing quietly on the free soil of Mars

THE END